DEATH ON A DUSTY STREET . . .

"No," he said, and at the time, Clint wasn't sure whether the man had made a move for his gun or not, but someone in the group fired a shot, and then the others started firing.

The man jerked about in the center of the street like a puppet on a string as the bullets struck his body. He didn't even step back, just jerked in place until they stopped firing, and then his riddled corpse fell to the ground.

*   *   *

SPECIAL PREVIEW!

Turn to the back of this book for an exciting excerpt from the magnificent new series . . .

RAILS WEST!

. . . the grand and epic story of the West's first railroads—and the brave men and women who forged an American dream.

DON'T MISS THESE
ALL-ACTION WESTERN SERIES
FROM THE BERKLEY PUBLISHING GROUP

THE GUNSMITH by J. R. Roberts
Clint Adams was a legend among lawmen, outlaws, and ladies. They called him . . . the Gunsmith.

LONGARM by Tabor Evans
The popular long-running series about U. S. Deputy Marshal Long—his life, his loves, his fight for justice.

LONE STAR by Wesley Ellis
The blazing adventures of Jessica Starbuck and the martial arts master, Ki. Over eight million copies in print.

SLOCUM by Jake Logan
Today's longest-running action western. John Slocum rides a deadly trail of hot blood and cold steel.

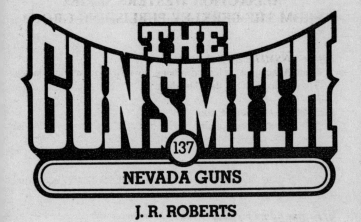

THE GUNSMITH

137

NEVADA GUNS

J. R. ROBERTS

JOVE BOOKS, NEW YORK

NEVADA GUNS

A Jove Book / published by arrangement with
the author

PRINTING HISTORY
Jove edition / May 1993

ISBN: 0-515-11105-8

Jove Books are published by The Berkley Publishing Group,
200 Madison Avenue, New York, New York 10016.
The name "JOVE" and the "J" logo
are trademarks belonging to Jove Publications, Inc.

PRINTED IN THE UNITED STATES OF AMERICA

10 9 8 7 6 5 4 3 2 1

ONE

When Clint Adams drove his rig into Allentown, Nevada, the secrets of Allentown were certainly not evident. If they had been, he might never have stopped. As it was, he liked the way the town looked. It was a fair-sized town, certainly no threat to Dodge City or Tombstone, but it looked like it had some growing to do.

Clint had been on the trail for more than a few days, and he was looking forward to a soft bed, a soft woman, and maybe some soft touches at a poker table. He would have settled for two out of three.

He found the livery and made arrangements for the rig, the team, and Duke, his big, black gelding. As was usually the case with an experienced liveryman, this fellow was properly appreciative of Duke and promised to take good care of him.

Clint tossed his saddlebags over his shoulder, hefted his rifle, and headed for one of Allentown's two hotels. He'd passed both on the way in, and it didn't matter to him which one he stayed in. They both looked like clean establishments.

1

The first one he came to was the Allen House. He could have guessed that one of the hotels would be called that. Idly, he wondered what the other one was called.

"Ah, a stranger in town," the desk clerk said loudly. Too loudly, Clint would think later.

The man was dressed in a white shirt, a bow tie, and a jacket that seemed a bit too small. His hair was slicked down and parted in the center.

"I'd like a room," Clint said.

"Certainly, sir," the clerk said. "Of course. Just sign the register, and I'll take good care of you."

Clint signed in as CLINT ADAMS, LABYRINTH, TEXAS. When the clerk turned the book around and read the name, he swallowed hard, and Clint knew that he had been recognized. He often considered signing in at hotels under some sort of alias—maybe the same one each time, maybe a different one, but that would make it difficult later if he had to admit who he was. Actually, he never wanted a town lawman to think he was trying to sneak into town. Clint Adams was his name, and he'd decided long ago that he'd have to live with the consequences of that.

"Yes, very good, sir," the clerk said. "Mr. Adams, I'll be givin' you room ten, best room in the house, sir."

"I don't want anything fancy or expensive," Clint told the man.

"Nothing expensive, sir. Same price as the rest of the rooms. I-it's just the b-best room we have."

"All right, then," Clint said. "I'll take it."

"Here's the key, sir."

The clerk's hand trembled slightly as he handed over the key.

"Thanks."

"Would you like someone to carry your bags, Mr. Adams?" the clerk asked.

"No," Clint said, picking up his rifle and saddlebags, "this is all I have. Thanks, anyway."

"Sure," the man said.

Clint was aware of the man's eyes on him as he went up the stairs. He could *feel* them, but he continued up the stairs without returning the look.

Upstairs he dropped his saddlebags on the bed, leaned his rifle against the wall, and then walked to the window. His room overlooked the main street, which was fine with him. It was also fine that there were no low rooftops or ledges or balconies outside his room. He didn't care to count the times someone had come through his window armed with more than just bad intentions.

While he was looking out the window, he saw the desk clerk hurrying down the street. The clerk had recognized him. It remained to be seen what kind of effect that was going to have on his stay.

TWO

Downstairs, after Clint Adams had gone up to his room, the clerk called over a replacement for him behind the desk and hurried from the hotel. He rushed down the street to the sheriff's office and entered without knocking.

Sheriff Marcus Bond looked up from his desk with a frown on his red, weathered face.

"What the hell—" he said.

"Sheriff—"

"What are you comin' bustin' in here for, Andy?" Bond demanded.

"Sheriff, I come to tell you—"

"How many times do I have to tell you to knock on my door?"

"Sheriff," Andy Gant said desperately, "I gotta tell you somethin'."

"My father's talkin' to you, Andy."

Andy turned to look at Red Bond, whom he hadn't seen when he came in. Red was the middle one of Marcus's three sons.

"Don't interrupt him."

Andy stared at Red. Even though Red wasn't as nas-

ty as his older brother, Ben, or as crazy as his younger
brother, George, he still scared Andy Gant.

"All right, Andy," Marcus Bond said, sitting back in
his chair, "go ahead. Tell me your big news."

"Uh . . ." Andy said, finding it hard to take his eyes
off Red, "a stranger just registered at the hotel, Sheriff."

"So?"

"So . . . he signed in as Clint Adams."

Bond sat forward and stared at Gant.

"Adams?"

"What's the matter, Pa?" Red asked.

"Clint Adams, you dummy," Bond said. He looked
at Andy and said, "All right, Andy, thanks. Get out."

"Yes, sir."

Once Andy Gant left, Red said, "You shouldn't call
me dummy in front of Andy, Pa."

"Shut up," Bond said. "Go find your brothers. I want
to talk to all three of you."

"About Clint Adams?"

"That's right."

"Who's Clint Adams?"

"Go find your brothers, Red!" Bond snapped.

"Okay, Pa, okay," Red said. "I'll go and find them."

As Red Bond left the office, Marcus Bond sat back and
ran his hand over his jaw. Since he had first become
sheriff of Allentown the town had been easy to hold
on to. No one who could be a danger to them had ever
come to town—until now.

Bond knew Clint Adams's reputation as the Gunsmith. The man could be a danger to them if he was
doing anything but passing through.

Marcus Bond was going to have to find out exactly
what Adams's intentions were.

• • •

Clint Adams sat on the bed in his hotel room and frowned. No doubt he'd be getting a visit from the town sheriff before long. The hotel clerk had obviously seen to that. The question was, why? Did the clerk inform the sheriff of the arrival of *every* stranger in town, or was it only because he recognized Clint's name?

Clint moved back to the window in time to see the desk clerk returning from the sheriff's office. The man was walking awkwardly, looking behind him as if he expected to be followed. Clint kept his eyes on the sheriff's office and before long saw another man step out. The badge on the man's chest reflected the sun. Clint had no way of knowing if the man was the sheriff or just the deputy.

The clerk, almost to the hotel, seemed to spot the man and in trying to walk even faster he tripped over his feet, almost sprawling into the street. He was obviously frightened—but why?

Clint watched the man with the badge, who stepped into the street and then crossed over and began to walk the other way, *away* from the hotel.

The visit from the law wasn't going to come right away, obviously, but it would come. It might have been a good idea to just leave town right then, but Clint decided against it. He was tired, and so was his team. Also, if he left now it would be for the wrong reasons. He decided to simply wait and see what the law had to say to him.

He decided to go and find a saloon and have a nice leisurely beer. After that, he could see about fulfilling his other two wants.

THREE

Red Bond knew where he'd find his older brother, Ben Bond. Meg Black had a small house at the northern end of town, and everyone in town knew that Meg was Ben's woman. Meg had resisted Ben in the beginning, but as far as Red was concerned, Ben had finally won Meg over.

Actually, that wasn't quite the way it was.

When the knock came at the door, Ben Bond sat up in bed. The move pulled the sheet off the woman who was lying next to him, her right arm flung across her eyes. He looked down at her and stared at her big breasts, which were flattened against her chest. Her nipples were big and brown, and one of them had a bloodstain on it. He had bitten through it, and even when she had cried out in pain, he had not stopped chewing on her.

"Somebody at the door," he said.

Dutifully, she removed her arm from her eyes, sat up, and got up off the bed. As he watched her walk across the room, her big buttocks undulating, he felt his penis begin to thicken again. She reached for her robe, but Ben Bond froze her with two words.

"Leave it!"

She turned and said, "Ben, I'm naked."

"So?"

"Ben," she said wearily, "someone is at the door."

"I know," Ben said. "That's what I said. Answer it."

"But Ben—"

"It's probably one of my brothers."

"I'm naked, Ben—"

"You ashamed of your body?"

"No, of course not—"

"Then answer the door, Meg," the man said coldly.

She knew from the sound of his voice that he was getting angry, and when he got angry sometimes he hurt her.

"All right," she said. What was the difference? she thought. She couldn't be any more degraded by this man than she was already.

She walked from the bedroom, across the living room to the front door. Through the lacy curtain over the door's window she could see Red Bond standing outside. Without pausing she reached for the doorknob and swung the door open. She stood there, her shoulders slumped, one hand on the door and the other on her hip. She could see Red's eyes widen and then grow hungry.

"What is it, Red?"

He had to lick his lips before he could reply.

"Pa wants Ben."

"I'll tell him."

"Uh . . . maybe I should tell him. . . ."

"I'll tell him, Red," Meg said. This Bond was the only one she didn't fear. She was afraid of George because he wasn't right in the head, and of Ben because he liked to hurt her. The father, though, Marcus, was the one that she feared the most because he controlled the other three.

"Meg—"

"Good-bye, Red," she said and closed the door in his face.

She walked back to the bedroom and stopped at the door.

"Who was it?" Ben asked. He was sitting at the bottom of his bed, still naked. His feet were wide apart, and she could see his penis standing up straight. She hoped that what she was about to tell him would cause it to shrivel.

"It was Red."

"What did he want?"

"He said that your father wants you."

Ben thought about that for a moment, then closed his left hand around his erection.

"Come here," he said thickly.

"Ben," she said, "he said your father wants you . . . now!"

She watched his eyes. If they stayed glazed then she knew that he was going to hurt her again, but if they cleared then she knew that he'd get dressed and leave. She watched him closely for several seconds, and then his sleepy eyes suddenly cleared.

"Shit!" he said.

Thank God, she thought.

FOUR

It took Red a little longer to find his younger brother, George, but he finally did. The youngest of the Bond boys was behind the livery stable with a small, whining dog.

"George?"

"What?"

"Pa wants you."

"I'll be there."

"He wants you now, George," Red said warily.

George looked up at his brother. Red saw the crazy look in his younger brother's eyes, but he didn't need that to know his brother was crazy. George was holding the dog pinned to the ground with his left hand, and the animal was making a whining sound. Its legs were moving, and its eyes were wild—almost as wild as the eyes of the man who was holding it— but it wasn't making a sound above the slight whine. In his right hand George Bond held a very sharp knife. He was holding it up so that the sun glinted off of it.

"I'll be there," George said slowly.

Red held his brother's eyes for a moment, then backed down.

"All right, George," Red said. "I'll tell 'im."

Red turned and walked away, and as he walked around to the side of the stable he heard a short yelp from the dog, and then nothing else. Shuddering, he started to walk faster.

FIVE

"Stranger?"

Clint looked at the bartender.

"How long have you been living in this town?" he asked the man.

The man looked startled by the question and then said, "Five years, I guess."

"You ever seen me before today?"

"Well . . . no."

"Then I guess I'm a stranger," Clint said. He took the beer that the man had poured for him and walked to a back table with it.

"Excuse me . . ." the bartender said to nobody, and started wiping the bar with a rag.

Clint wasn't sure why he had bitten the bartender's head off, except that he was already annoyed. He had been in town only a short while, spoken only to the desk clerk, and already he had felt pressure. Maybe it was imagined pressure. Maybe the law *wouldn't* come looking for him. Maybe the clerk had run to the sheriff to talk about something else. Only time would tell.

The saloon was nearly empty since it was early in the day. There were a couple of other men seated alone at tables and two men at the bar, but that was it. He looked around and didn't see any gaming tables in the room. That suited him. He would prefer to get up his own poker game than have to play a house-run game. He tried the beer and found it good and cold. It cut through the trail dust in his throat, and he didn't stop until half of it was gone.

The bartender tossed him furtive glances in between swipes at the bar. The man was big and beefy, and yet he managed to look like a child who had been chastised. All that was missing was the pushed-out lower lip. Clint almost felt like getting up and apologizing to the man, but he quelled the urge. Maybe—*maybe*—he would apologize when he went up to get his second beer.

Marcus Bond looked up as his middle son, Red, reentered the office.

"Did you find them?"

"Yeah, Pa."

"Where?"

"Ben was with Meg."

"That woman . . ." Marcus said, shaking his head. "Is he coming?"

"She said she'd tell him."

Marcus glared at Red and said, "*You* didn't tell him I wanted him?"

"She answered the door, Pa," Red said.

"You should have gone in."

"She wouldn't let me."

Something in Marcus Bond's face made Red stop in his tracks on his way to the coffeepot.

"What?" Red asked.

"A *woman* wouldn't let you into her house?" Marcus asked.

"Pa," Red said, "she's not just a woman; she's *Ben's* woman."

"She's still just a woman, Red," Marcus said. "No woman tells a Bond what to do. Do you understand?"

"Sure, Pa, sure I understand."

"If Ben isn't here in five minutes, you're goin' back to get him."

"All right, Pa," Red said, "whatever you say."

"Did you find George?"

Red hesitated, then said, "Yeah," and continued on to the coffeepot.

"Well?"

"Well what?" Red asked without looking at his father. Instead he concentrated heavily on pouring himself a cup of coffee.

"Red?"

"Yeah, Pa?"

"Look at me, damn it!"

Red almost spilled his coffee as he turned to look at his father.

"Was he doin' it again?" Marcus asked.

"Doin' what, Pa?"

"You know what, Red," Marcus said. "Was he butcherin' another dog?"

"Uh . . . yeah, he was, Pa."

"Jesus," Marcus Bond said, closing his eyes. "I don't know which one of them boys is worse, Ben with his women or George with his . . ."

"Yeah, Pa."

Marcus opened his eyes and glared at Red.

"Or you."

Red looked surprised and hurt.

"Me, Pa?" Red said. "What did I do?"

"Nothin', Red," Marcus said. "That's the problem. You never do nothin'."

"I do what you tell me, Pa," Red Bond said, the hurt evident in his tone.

Just for a moment Marcus Bond's face softened.

"Yeah," he said, "you do that, boy, you do that. Pour me a cup of coffee, will ya?"

"Sure, Pa," Red said, "sure."

SIX

When Ben Bond entered his father's office, Marcus said, "Sit down and shut up."

Ben was used to being spoken to in this manner. It did not bother him. He walked to the coffeepot and poured himself a drink. When he looked at his brother, he did not acknowledge Red's shrug.

They waited about fifteen more minutes—in total silence—before George Bond entered. There was blood on his hands.

"Jesus," Marcus said, "the least you could do is wash the blood off your hands before you come into the office."

George gave his father an unconcerned look, then started to lift his hand to his mouth.

"You lick that blood off your hands, George, and I'll give you the worst whippin' I've ever given you—and you know I can do it."

There was tension in the air as father and son stared at each other. George, twenty-three, had no expression on his face. Marcus Bond, in his mid-fifties, was breathing heavily and was red in the face.

George was as tall as his father, but was a good forty pounds lighter. Both Ben and Red knew that their father could do what he said. Red hoped that it wouldn't happen. Ben was quietly urging George to go ahead and do it. He wanted to see the crazy little shit get a beating.

"Go and wash it off," Marcus said quietly. He had managed to control his temper, which *everyone* in the room knew was rare. "We'll wait."

George walked into the back where the cells were, and they heard him dipping his hands in a bucket of water. When he came back, his hands were at his sides, and they were dripping. He hadn't bothered to dry them.

"All right," Marcus said, addressing his three sons, "Clint Adams is in town."

He looked at all of them, and they in turn looked back at him.

"Does that name mean anything to anyone?"

"Sure," Ben said. "He's the Gunsmith. You want us to run him out of town?"

"I might," Marcus said, "I just might, but that would be askin' for trouble."

"He won't be no trouble, Pa," Ben said. "I could take him alone, if you let me."

"Don't be an ass!"

Ben gave his father a sharp look.

"You don't think I can do it?"

"I know you can't," Marcus said. "If we do have to run him out of town, we'll do it together."

"When, Pa?" Red asked.

"I'll decide that," Marcus said, "after I talk to the man."

Ben put his cup down and stood up straight.

"I'll go with you."

"Fine," Marcus said. "I wanted one of you to go with me, anyway—but you'll let me do all of the talkin'."

"Sure, Pa," Ben said. "Don't we always?"

Marcus didn't answer.

"Come on," he said, standing up and grabbing his hat. "Let's go and find him."

As Marcus and Ben went out the door, Red realized that would leave him alone with his crazy brother, George.

"I, uh, I guess I better go and do some rounds," he said, hurrying to the door. He left and closed the door behind him without looking back at his brother.

Once he was alone, George raised his right wrist to his mouth and started to lick the blood from his wrist, where he had made sure *not* to wash it off.

SEVEN

Marcus and Ben Bond checked the hotel first, and when they didn't find Clint Adams there, they went to Allentown's only saloon.

Clint was still seated at the back table, with a second beer. He had collected it without apologizing to the bartender.

"That him?" Ben asked.

"Must be," Marcus said. "Come on—and remember to keep your mouth shut."

"Sure, Pa. . . ."

Marcus led the way to the table. . . .

Clint saw the two men enter and saw the badges on their chests. Neither was the man he had seen earlier, but he knew now that man had been a deputy.

The older man, broad-chested, in his fifties, was the sheriff. The other man, younger but built along the same lines, was a deputy, but Clint had the feeling he was also looking at father and son. He wondered if the other deputy was also a son.

He sat back in his chair as they approached him,

keeping his left hand on the beer mug while allowing his right to dangle down toward the floor.

"Clint Adams?" the older man asked.

"That's right."

For a moment the two men eyed each other, taking one another's measure.

"My name's Marcus Bond," the man finally said. "I'm the sheriff of Allentown."

Clint hesitated, then said, "Glad to meet you. Do we have some business, Sheriff?"

"We might."

"Maybe you should sit down, then," Clint said, indicating the chair across from him.

The sheriff hesitated, then pulled the chair out and sat down opposite Clint. Clint turned his attention to the deputy, who was still standing. The man had cold eyes and an expressionless face.

"This is my deputy," the sheriff said, "and my son, Ben."

Clint nodded, and Ben nodded back. The younger Bond's face looked dead—especially his eyes.

"Ben," Marcus said, "go and stand by the bar."

"Pa—"

"Ben!" Marcus said sharply, and then added in an easier tone, "Have a beer."

Clint could see that the younger man did not like being dismissed, but ultimately he obeyed and moved over to the bar. Clint watched as the bartender immediately—and hurriedly—set a beer on the bar near the man's elbow and then moved away from him.

"What can I do for you, Sheriff?" Clint asked, turning his attention back to the sheriff.

"I like to check on all strangers that come into town," Marcus Bond said.

"So go ahead, check," Clint said, with a shrug. "Can I get you a beer?"

"Not right now," Bond said. "What brings you to Allentown, Mr. Adams?"

Something wasn't right, here. Sheriff Bond did not strike Clint as being a polite man, and yet here he was, being polite.

"I'm just passing through, Sheriff," Clint said. "I drive a rig, and my team needs a little rest. We've been on the trail for a while."

"Headin' anywhere in particular?" Bond asked.

"That's just it," Clint said. "I'm not. I'm just riding around, doing some gunsmithing—"

"You mean, you're a real gunsmith?" The man sounded genuinely surprised.

"That's right."

"Well," Bond said, looking interested, "I always thought it was just, you know . . . a name . . . a reputation."

"I like to work on guns, Sheriff," Clint said simply. It wasn't much of a reply, but he didn't particularly want to say anything more about names and reputations.

"So you can fix 'em as well as handle 'em, huh?" Bond asked.

"I suppose that's true."

"Then you'll be lookin' for some . . . business here?" the lawman asked.

"If somebody needs a gun fixed," Clint said, "I'll be available."

"How long do you plan on stayin' in Allentown, then?" Bond asked.

"I'm not sure," Clint said. "A few days, I guess . . . that is, unless you have some reason why I *shouldn't* stay in town?"

"No," Bond said, shaking his head, "not that I can think of right now. In fact, if you're lookin' to work on some guns, I might even have some business to give you myself."

"Sure, Sheriff," Clint said. "For you there'd be no charge."

"That's nice of you," Bond said, without smiling. In fact, as polite as he had been up to that point, there was never a *hint* of a smile on his face.

"Anything else?" Clint asked.

"I'd just like you to watch yourself while you're in town," Bond said. "There might be some people around who know your reputation. They, uh, might want to try you out—if you know what I mean."

"I'm aware of that, Sheriff," Clint said, "and I always try to watch my step."

"That's good," Bond said. "That's real good."

The two men stared at each other, and Clint found something . . . deadly about the man. He wasn't *just* a town sheriff.

"Tell me," Clint said, "do you have any other deputies, besides your son?"

"Actually," Bond said, "I have three deputies, and they're all my sons. That there at the bar is Ben, my oldest. I've also got Red, my middle boy, and George, my youngest."

"I see," Clint said. "Then it's a real family effort, huh?"

"They're good boys," Bond said. Somehow, Clint doubted it.

"No other children?"

"I have a daughter," Bond said, and then rose without elaborating as to her name or where she might be.

"I'm a little curious about something, Sheriff," Clint said.

"What's that?"

"How long have you been a lawman?"

"Actually," Bond said, "I was never a lawman until I came to Allentown."

"And when was that?"

"About a year ago," Bond said. "I don't think I have any more questions for you, Mr. Adams, and I think our little talk has put my mind to rest."

"About why I'm here, you mean?"

"That's right."

"You mean, now you're sure I'm not here looking for trouble?"

"I *was* a little concerned when I heard you were here," Bond admitted. "That's only natural, given your reputation, don't you think?"

"I can see how it might be, yes."

"So I guess I'll be seeing you around town then," Bond said.

"I suppose so."

"Enjoy your stay in Allentown."

"Thanks."

The sheriff turned and walked to the batwing doors and went out without a glance back at Clint, or at his deputy son.

Ben Bond put his beer mug down carefully, gave Clint a long hard stare, and then followed his father out of the saloon.

Clint sat back with his beer mug in his hand and had the feeling he had just watched a masterful performance. Marcus Bond had played the dutiful sheriff very well, but Clint had a feeling that the man he had just met was far from the *real* Marcus Bond.

EIGHT

Outside Ben caught up to his father and fell into step with him.

"Did you tell him, Pa?"

Marcus Bond answered without looking at his son.

"Tell him what?"

"To leave town."

"No, Ben," Bond said, "I did not tell him to leave town."

"Why not?"

"Because," Marcus Bond said, "I didn't have any reason to."

"Why do we need a reason, Pa?" Ben asked. "It's our town. We can do anything we want with it. We can chase anyone we want *out*."

Marcus Bond stopped walking abruptly, and Ben actually went on a step or two before he realized it. The younger man stopped and turned to face his father, who was staring at him impatiently.

"Think for a minute, Ben," the elder Bond said. "If I tell Clint Adams to leave, for no reason, he's gonna wonder why."

"So?"

24

"Why am I tryin' to explain this to you?" Marcus said. "So if he rides out of town on his own, I'll prefer it that way."

"I won't," Ben Bond said. "I want to try him, Pa. I can take him, I know I can."

Marcus Bond simply stared at his son, shaking his head to himself.

"Just do what you're told, Ben, and don't try to think," Marcus Bond said. "Okay? Everything will be just fine if you and your brothers will just do what I tell you to do."

Marcus started walking again. Ben hesitated. For the first time in his life, Ben Bond wondered if his father was getting old.

Clint remained in the saloon for some time after the meeting with Marcus Bond, thinking the situation over. The sheriff hadn't exactly warned him out of town— or even *warned* him at all—but there was something menacing about the man, something unspoken. How could a man like that be elected sheriff of Allentown?

Clint eyed the bartender for a moment and recalled how frightened the man had looked in the presence of Marcus Bond and his son, Ben. Maybe he'd be able to tell Clint something about Sheriff Marcus Bond—if Clint phrased the questions right.

He stood up and walked to the bar.

"Another beer," he said.

"Sure."

The bartender drew the beer and set it in front of him without looking at him.

"About before," Clint said. "I'm sorry I snapped at you like that."

The bartender looked at him now, in surprise.

"Uh, hey, that's okay," the man said. "Some days you got to snap at somebody."

"Ain't that the truth?" Clint said. "So that was your sheriff, huh?"

"Oh, yeah," the bartender said. "Sheriff Bond."

"And his son?"

"Three deputies," the bartender said, "three sons."

"Is he a good sheriff?" Clint asked.

"I guess so," the man said with a shrug.

"And his sons? Are they good deputies?"

"I guess," the man said, again with a shrug. He offered nothing else. Instead he asked, "Are you really the Gunsmith?"

"I guess so," Clint said with a shrug. He sipped the third beer, paid for all three, and left.

NINE

Clint walked from the saloon to the newspaper office, which he found after asking a small boy for directions. He thanked the boy and gave him two bits. The boy clutched the coin tightly in his hand and bounded away happily.

The newspaper was called *The Allentown Gazette*, which was written on the plate glass window in what looked like gold leaf. It was also written on the glass of the front door, but in plain white paint. He opened the door and entered without knocking.

Inside he was assailed by the smell of ink and the sound of a printing press. Had he knocked, no one would have heard him anyway.

He stopped just inside the door, closing it behind him, and looked around. For a moment he thought he was alone in the room and that the press might be running wild on its own, but then he saw a head behind the press. Just the top of it, a blond crescent bobbing into view every so often. Suddenly, the person straightened up, and he saw that it was a woman.

27

She noticed him just a moment after he saw her, and she stopped short, obviously startled. He saw her mouth open then but couldn't hear what she was saying.

"What?"

"Sound . . . you . . ." he heard this time, but still couldn't hear her clearly.

He shook his head, indicating that he still could not make out what she was saying.

She came out from behind the press, and he got a better look at her. She was wearing a shirt and a pair of jeans, both of which were too big for her. In fact, the jeans were held around her waist with a piece of string. Her blond hair was pulled back from her face and tied with a ribbon. Her face was smudged with both dirt and ink, and her hands were black—as was the cloth she was wiping them on as she approached him.

"I asked you how it sounds to you?" he heard her ask.

"Loud," he replied.

"Too loud," Clint thought he heard her say. "God-damned thing!" She looked at him and said, "I'm trying to fix it. I know how to use it, but I don't really know how to fix it."

"Can't you get someone—" he started to shout, but she waved him off and then put her hand up for him to wait a moment.

She went back around behind the press and hit a switch, and abruptly the thing stopped and the noise abated. She came back around, wiping her hands on the cloth again.

"My husband was the one who could make the damned thing sing," she said.

"Can't he fix it now?"

"Be kind of hard," she said. "He's dead."

"I'm sorry."

"Don't be," she said. "He died three months ago, and left me all of this. That's enough right there for me to curse his memory."

Clint didn't know what to say.

"Sorry if I'm shocking you," she said. "My name's Hailey Morgan. Owner, publisher, and only reporter on *The Allentown Gazette*." She put her hand out for him to shake, then looked at it and withdrew it, saying, "Sorry."

"That's all right," he said. "I guess it's a dirty job, but someone's got to do it."

She stared at him for a moment, then smiled and said, "Hey, that's pretty good."

"Thanks."

Suddenly, a look came over her face that indicated she had just thought of something horrible.

"Jesus," she said.

"What?"

She laughed nervously and said, "I must look like sh—I must look terrible."

"I wouldn't say that," Clint said.

Through all of the dirt and the ink and the layers of clothing he got the impression that he was looking at an attractive woman in her late thirties. She could have been a few years younger, or a few years older. He'd be able to tell better if he ever saw her clean.

"Hell," she said, lifting a hand to her hair. "Well, can't do anything about it now. What can I do for you, Mr.—"

"Adams," he said, "my name is Clint Adams."

"I know that name from somewhere," she said.

"Do you?"

"Probably saw it in the papers a few times, huh?" she asked.

"You might have," he admitted.

"Well, Mr. Adams," Hailey Morgan said, "what can I do for you?"

"I just rode into town today," he said, "and I met your sheriff."

Hailey Morgan frowned.

"He's not *my* sheriff, that's for damn sure," she said.

"Well . . . I find myself a little curious about the man, and his sons."

"Did you meet his sons?"

"Just one of them," he said. "I believe his name was Ben?"

"That's the oldest," Hailey said, her face betraying her intense distaste for the man. "What is it you'd like to know about Sheriff Bond and his sons?"

"Well . . . I wanted to look at copies of your newspaper from last year, when he was elected."

"Why?"

"I just find it hard to believe that the man I met was elected by a town to be its sheriff."

"You're very perceptive," she said.

"What do you mean?"

"I mean you're right," she said. "He wasn't elected to be sheriff."

"But he *is* sheriff," Clint said, a little puzzled. "Was he hired by the town council?"

"Nope," she said, shaking her head. "He wasn't elected, and he wasn't hired."

Clint frowned.

"There's no other option," he said. "He had to be either elected or hired."

"There is one other option," she said.

"And what's that?"

"He took it," she said.

"Took it?"

She nodded.

"He rode into town, was here a week, decided that he wanted to be sheriff, and he just . . . *took* the job."

TEN

It surprised both Hailey Morgan and Clint himself when he asked her if she could take a break for lunch.

"I'll have to get cleaned up," she warned, "*and* change."

"Where do you live?"

"Upstairs."

He shrugged and said, "I'll wait."

"Okay," she said. "I'll be right back."

Of course, she *wasn't* right back. It was a good half hour before she finally returned, but it was certainly worth the wait.

She hadn't put on anything fancy, just a shirt and jeans that actually fit, but cleaned up, with her hair down instead of swept away from her face, she presented an entirely different picture than the one he had first seen.

She had done nothing to her face but wash it, but that had been enough. Hailey Morgan—probably around thirty-five years old—was a lovely woman. There were some lines at the corners of her eyes and her mouth, but they did nothing to detract from the fact that she was an attractive woman, and Clint found himself quite glad that he had decided to check out the local newspaper.

"Ready?" she asked. Was she nervous? She wasn't looking directly at him, and she rubbed her palms over her thighs, as if drying them.

"I'm ready," he said. "Let's go to lunch."

"I know a place . . ." she said as they left the office.

Across the street, as Clint and Hailey Morgan left the newspaper office, Red Bond was walking by. When he saw Clint and Hailey, he stopped short and stared. He knew that his father, Marcus, was sweet on the lady newspaper editor. It wasn't anything like the way Ben felt about Meg Black. In fact, Red knew that his father and Hailey Morgan had never even had a meal together, but he also knew that his father wasn't going to like hearing that he had seen Adams and Hailey together.

And, of course, he *would* tell him.

Hailey saw Red and said under her breath, "Oh, shit."

"What is it?" Clint asked.

"Don't look," she said. "Red Bond is across the street, watching us."

"Red?"

"He's the sheriff's middle son," Hailey said.

"And does that concern you, that he saw us together?" Clint asked. "Are you and he—"

"God, no!" Hailey said quickly. "I wouldn't be caught dead with *any* of those men."

"Then what is it?"

"Well, I don't want to sound . . . immodest," she said, "but Red is undoubtedly going to tell his father that he saw us together."

"And?"

"And . . . I think Sheriff Bond . . . um, likes me."
When she said it her voice shook, as if the concept
either frightened her or sickened her.

"You think?"

"Well . . . he hasn't come out and *said* it in so many
words," she said, "but a woman can sort of tell when
a man finds her . . . attractive."

"Well," Clint said, "I suppose that means I might be
talking to the sheriff again sooner than I thought."

"Maybe," Hailey Morgan said, "you should just leave
town."

"I don't think so," Clint said, taking her elbow, "at
least, not before we have lunch."

ELEVEN

Hailey took Clint to one of those small, family-owned cafés he had run into in so many towns. They were usually run by husbands and wives—or on occasions brothers and sisters, or sisters and sisters—with the labor divided up evenly.

This one was run by two sisters, one of whom showed Hailey and Clint to a table. The woman had a round, pleasant face, but was very fat. After the woman left them at their table, Hailey leaned forward and told Clint in a conspiratorial whisper that her name was Eden and that her sister, Ellen, was even fatter.

"That's a shame," Clint said. "If she lost weight, she'd be quite pretty."

"Do you think so?"

"I know so."

Hailey thought that over for a moment, then said slowly, "Yes, I suppose she would be—and Ellen, too. I'll bet no other man has taken the time to notice that—or any other women, for that matter. *I* didn't notice it until you mentioned it."

"Don't make anything out of it," he said. "It was just an observation."

"An astute one," she said. "I'm impressed."

Clint waved her compliment aside.

"Why did you want to have lunch with me?" she asked him.

His answer was interrupted by the reappearance of Eden with a pot of coffee.

"Work on this while I get your order," she said.

"We haven't ordered yet," Clint said.

Hailey smiled, and Eden said, "Hailey has the same thing almost every night. I'll bring you the same as her, if it's all right?"

"Sure," Clint said immediately. "If she has it every night, it must be good."

"It is," Eden said. "My sister Ellen is a great cook. There's nobody better."

"Except maybe you," Hailey said to Eden. Clint could tell that Hailey was studying Eden's face.

"Don't tell Ellen," Eden said, then left them to their coffee.

"You know, you're right," Hailey said. "About her face, I mean."

"Not only her face," he said. "Her body, too."

Hailey sat back and stared at him.

"Clint," she said, "I—can I call you Clint?"

"I prefer it."

"Clint, I *like* Eden, but she's . . ."—Hailey leaned forward and whispered—"fat. There's not much you can do about that."

"She's heavy," Clint said, "not fat. Look at her when she comes out. Fat people are soft and sloppy. This woman is not. I don't know about her sister, but Eden is heavy, not fat."

Hailey frowned and sat forward.

"Maybe we'd better get back to the subject."

"Which was what?"

"Why we're having lunch?"

"Because you're the newspaper publisher," he said, "and you can probably tell me more from memory—and facts—than anyone else in this town."

"About Marcus Bond?"

"And his brood."

"Ah," she said, "the daughter."

"That's right," Clint said, "he told me had a daughter, but he didn't seem to want to talk about her."

"Of course not."

"Why not?"

"Because she's the only member of the family who's decent," Hailey said. "I don't know how she got stuck with him as a father and them as brothers."

"I haven't seen her," Clint said.

"That's because they keep her in their house."

"Their house?"

"The one they stole from the last sheriff before they rode him out of town."

"Well," Clint said, "at least they didn't kill him."

"No," she said, "but they would have, if he hadn't left."

"Did he have family?"

"No," she said. "That was the only good thing about the incident."

"What about his deputies?"

"They left after he did," she said. "They weren't about to go up against Marcus Bond and his sons for five dollars a month—or whatever they were being paid."

Clint frowned.

"I don't think I'd ever heard of Bond and his sons before I came here."

"You hadn't," she said. "I checked them out after they took over. They weren't wanted for anything that I could find out."

"And what about your town council?" Clint asked. "They went along with this? Bond appointing himself the sheriff of Allentown?"

"They and all the other men in town," Hailey said. "They're all afraid of the Bonds. They were then, and they are now."

"And what *about* now?" he asked. "How do the people in town feel about their law?"

She shrugged.

"I think most of them have come to accept Marcus and his sons as the law in Allentown. And you want to know something? They keep the peace, they really do—except for those times that *they* feel like breaking it."

"Like how?"

"Oh . . . little things, I guess," she said. "For instance, they don't pay for *anything* in town. Meals, drinks, guns, bullets . . . *women* . . . they don't pay for a thing."

"The merchants go along with that, huh?"

"Every one of them," Hailey said.

Clint looked around and said, "Even here?"

"That's funny," she said.

"What is?"

"They tried to eat here, and Eden and Ellen won't serve them," she said. "Not after the first time they came and wouldn't pay up."

"And they stood for that?"

She nodded, smiling.

"Marcus told his boys to stay away from here," Hailey

said. "It's the only thing about the Bonds I can't figure out."

"Maybe they're just afraid of Eden and Ellen," Clint suggested.

Hailey laughed and said, "Wouldn't that be something?"

Eden appeared with two plates heaped with steaks and vegetables, and Clint and Hailey put off their conversation until they had made a dent in the feast.

TWELVE

Marcus Bond listened in silence to the news his son, Red, was bringing him. Off to one side Ben also listened, and when his brother finished, it was Ben who spoke first.

"So?" he said. "Adams went to talk to the lady editor. What's that got to do with us?"

Marcus turned his head and looked at Ben.

"What do you suppose he's talking to her about?" he asked his oldest son.

"I don't know," Ben said, scowling. "Ink?"

Marcus shook his head and said, "How did I get saddled with you three?"

"What did I do?" Red asked.

"You?" Marcus asked, turning his attention to his middle son. "You came runnin' over here with this news like I was gonna go into some kind of jealous rage or somethin'. What's wrong with you boys? Don't you realize that Adams is talkin' to Hailey Morgan about us?"

Ben and Red exchanged a long glance, and then Red said, "I knew that."

"Yeah, sure," Ben said.

"Shut up, both of you," Marcus Bond said. "I've got to think."

"Fine," Ben said, heading for the door. "You think. I got things to do."

As Ben went out the door, Marcus shouted, "Stay away from Adams until I say different, Ben!"

"He ain't goin' near Adams, Pa," Red said.

"No? What's he doin', then?"

"He's goin' over to Meg Black's house."

"Shit," Marcus Bond said grumpily, "I knew that. . . ."

After lunch Clint asked for another pot of coffee, which was excellent. Hot and strong, it complemented the meal, which was as good as any Clint had ever had. He had found some fine restaurants during his travels, but the best ones were usually these small cafés in small, western towns. They were often better than most of the restaurants he had been to in places like San Francisco, Denver, and New York.

When he told this to Eden, she blushed and thanked him and told him that she would tell her sister he said so.

"Would I be able to meet your sister and tell her myself?" he asked.

"Oh, I'm afraid not," Eden said.

"Why not?" Clint asked, aware that Hailey was smiling across the table at him.

Eden leaned forward, as if about to impart some great secret to him, and said, "She's fat. It makes her shy."

"Oh," he said, "I see. Well, you'll thank her for me anyway, won't you?"

"I will."

As Eden went back to the kitchen, Hailey laughed out loud at him.

"Now let's see you convince Ellen that she's not fat," she said.

"Maybe we should just leave before I have to do that," Clint said.

"All right," Hailey said.

Outside they started walking back toward the newspaper office.

"So what do you intend to do?" she asked.

"I don't know," he said. "I stopped here to get some rest."

"And ran into an unexpected situation," she said. "No one would blame you if you just left town and never looked back."

"I guess not," Clint said, "but if I did that, I'd feel like I had been run out."

"So?" she asked. "Once Marcus realizes that you're here, and realizes *who* you are—oh yes, I know who you are; I was just too polite to make a fuss about it."

"I appreciate it."

"Marcus will make a fuss, though," she said. "Or more to the point, Ben will."

"Not if I don't," Clint said.

"That's not true, I'm afraid," she said. "If you stay, it will become unbearable for Marcus Bond. He'll wonder why you're staying, and whether or not you're going to try to go against him."

"And his three boys?" he asked. "Four to one odds is not my idea of a favorable condition."

They reached the newspaper office where she stopped and turned to face him.

"Mark my words, Clint," she said. "If you stay, you'll have to face those four to one odds sooner or later. Get out while the gettin' is good."

"I'll think about it," he promised.

"I hope you leave," she said, "but if you don't . . . maybe we can have dinner together."

He smiled and said, "I'll have to let you know."

She gave him a slow smile, then turned and went back into her office to wrestle with her old printing press.

Abruptly, he wondered if he would be mentioned in the very next edition of *The Allentown Gazette*.

THIRTEEN

Clint walked over to the livery stable to check on his team, and on Duke. The liveryman paid him no mind as he went over his animals, checking their condition, paying special attention to the big, black gelding.

When he was finished he walked around the stable instead of going right back to town. He had some thinking to do. Come morning he could hitch up his team and leave Allentown and its peculiar brand of law behind. The town was virtually enslaved by Marcus Bond and his sons, but what business was that of his? The townspeople certainly weren't doing anything to change their situation, so why should he worry about it? Even an intelligent woman like Hailey Morgan was tolerating it, living with it, operating a business within it—although she apparently had very little to do with them, other than being an object of the sheriff's affection, albeit from a distance, but how long would *that* last?

When Clint reached the back of the stable, he stopped short. He saw a carcass on the ground. Someone had slit the throat of a small dog, and then gutted it and left it for the flies.

"Hey!" he called out to the liveryman, banging on the rear door of the stable.

It took a few moments, but the man finally appeared.

"What can I do for ya?"

"Who did this?" Clint asked, indicating the dog.

"Can't say as I rightly saw who did it," the liveryman said, scratching the stubble on his face.

"You didn't *see* who did it," Clint said, interpreting the man's carefully chosen words, "but you *know* who did it, don't you?"

"Why you want to know, mister?"

"I like dogs," Clint said. "Now who did it?"

"Well . . . they's only one feller in town who *likes* cuttin' up animals . . . that I know of, that is."

"And who might that be?"

"You, uh, ain't gonna say where you heard this, are you?" the man asked.

"No," Clint said. "Who is it?"

"His name's Bond," the man said.

"One of the sheriff's sons?"

"Only Bonds hereabouts that I know of."

"Which son?" Clint asked.

"The youngest."

"I know of Ben and Red. Either of them the youngest?" Clint asked.

The man shook his head.

"This'n's George."

Clint looked down at the dog.

"What's wrong with George?" he asked.

The man shrugged his bony shoulders and said, "Just ain't right in the head, if you know what I mean."

"Uh-huh," Clint said, "and I suppose his brothers *are* right in the head?"

"Don't know about that," the man said. "I jest know

they don't go around cuttin' up cats and dogs and other small critters."

"Probably pulls the wings off of flies, too," Clint said.

"Wouldn't surprise me none."

"You got a shovel?"

"What fer?"

"I'm going to bury the dog."

The man stared at Clint for a few seconds, then shrugged his shoulders and said, "Suit yerself. Yeah, I got a shovel. I'll get it."

Clint waited for the man to return with the shovel. He knew it was stupid to stay in town and risk having to face Marcus Bond and his sons just because of a dead dog, but since there were no *smart* reasons to do it, this one would have to do.

FOURTEEN

While she was working on her printing press, Hailey Morgan couldn't stop thinking about Clint Adams. She had met a lot of men in her life, both before and after the death of her husband, and Clint Adams was the first she had found interesting in a long time—*including* her husband. When she caught her finger in the damned press because she was thinking about him instead of about what she was doing, she decided to give up. Let the damned thing run noisy—or noisier than it should, anyway.

She went to her desk and sat looking at her stories for this edition. She only put out two editions a week, because what the hell was there to write about? Now she had something big she could write about, but did she dare? Clint had taken her to lunch to ask *her* questions, not to end up the subject of an article in her newspaper. How would he feel if he read about himself in the next edition—due out tomorrow?

She knew how he'd feel—angry. And then she'd have the only interesting man she'd met in years mad at her—but she'd have a hell of a story for the paper. THE

GUNSMITH COMES TO ALLENTOWN TO CLEAN IT UP.

Hell, she thought, if only that were true, but if she printed it that way, it would be nothing but a bald-faced lie made up to sell newspapers.

If, however, Clint decided to stay in Allentown for a while, a clash with the Bonds would be inevitable— and wouldn't *that* be something to write about!

Meg Black lay on her side, listening to Ben Bond snore. It was the most beautiful sound she had ever heard, because it meant he was asleep, and that meant that he wouldn't be touching her.

Slowly, trying desperately not to wake him, she slid from her bed, padded on bare feet to her dresser, opened it, and took out her gun. She had bought it a long time ago for protection and had never fired it, except in practice. Of course, she had never hit anything, but she had pulled the trigger enough times to know that she could do that.

She carried the gun back to the bed, where she stood and pointed it at Ben Bond's back. She stood that way for a few moments, then turned, went back to the dresser, put the gun away, and returned to the bed.

That must have been the fiftieth or even one hundredth time she had done that. Ben Bond would never know how close he had come to death all those times. Soon, she promised herself, curling up into a ball, one day soon she would work up the nerve to pull the trigger, and then face up to the consequences of her actions . . . gladly.

Nancy Bond pushed aside the lace curtain on the front window of the house and peered outside. Her father was not in sight, and neither were any of her brothers. She breathed a sigh of relief.

Nancy was twenty, the youngest of Marcus Bond's offspring. She cooked for them, and cleaned, and sewed, and had been doing so ever since she could remember. Thank God there was never any shortage of women around for men like her father and brothers, so she had never had to . . . to do *that*.

The rest, however, was bad enough. She pushed aside the curtain and looked out again. They were nowhere in sight. All she had to do was slip from the house, start walking, and never stop. That's all. What was so hard about that?

One day—one day *soon*—she promised herself, she would do it.

FIFTEEN

After he buried the dog, Clint walked over to the newspaper office to talk some more to Hailey Morgan about the Bond family. As he entered he couldn't help noticing that the printing press was operating. It sounded even more noisy than it had earlier.

He looked around and saw Hailey sitting at a desk against the wall. He opened his mouth to shout, but stopped when he realized that she wouldn't hear him.

He walked across the room and stopped behind her. She was still unaware of him and continued to write. He assumed she was working on a story and peered over her shoulder. It was a little hard to miss his own name, since it had been written several times, with THE GUNSMITH in block letters.

He tapped her on the shoulder. She turned her head quickly and stared at him, her eyes wide.

"You scared me," she said. He read her lips more than heard her.

He pointed to the press and mouthed, "Shut it off."

She nodded, got up and shut off the press. Then she turned and faced him. He didn't look at her. Instead, he looked at the story she was writing. It was all about how Clint Adams, the Gunsmith, had come into town and rescued it from the iron grip of self-appointed Sheriff Marcus Bond and his sons.

He turned and looked at her. She had the good grace to look sheepish.

"Writing fiction now?" he asked.

"Clint—"

"Actually, it's better than some of the dime novel stuff I've read about myself."

"Clint, let me explain—"

"Okay," he said, folding his arms. "Explain."

"I was just writing that," she said, pointing to the desk, "so I'd have at least *part* of it ready . . ."

"Part of it?"

"Well, yes," she said, "I mean, I don't know *how* you're going to rescue the town from Sheriff Bond—"

"The *iron grip* of Sheriff Bond and his sons, I think was the way you put it." He turned, as if to read it again to be sure.

"Um, yes, well . . . like I said, I just want to be ready."

"You're just assuming that I'll stay and fight the Bonds for the benefit of the town, right?"

She hesitated, then said, "Not assumed, so much as . . . hoped?"

"If I'm going to do that," he said, "I mean, if I'm going to *consider* doing that, we're going to have to . . . talk some more."

"About them?" she asked. "The Bonds, I mean."

"Well," he said, "we can certainly start with them."

She folded her arms and stared at him speculatively for a few moments, until she was sure that he meant what she thought he meant.

"Why don't we go upstairs?" she suggested.

• • •

Upstairs turned out to be two rooms, one of which had a comfortable-looking bed in it. As they entered she took his hand and led him to the bed. Once there she turned and leaned into him.

She had her hair pinned back again, and he took the time to unpin it. Once it was down he took two handfuls of it and pulled her face to his so he could kiss her, softly at first, then more insistently.

She responded instantly to his kisses, thrusting her tongue into his mouth. She wrapped her arms around him, pressing her palms to his back and grinding her hips against him.

They kissed until they were breathless, and then Clint began to undress her.

"I can do this," she said, pushing him away gently. "Undress yourself."

Obviously she felt strongly about that, so he stepped back even farther and they each undressed themselves. He'd ask her about this later, about why she didn't want him to undress her.

When they were naked they took the time to look at each other. He was pleased by what he saw. She was strongly built, solid breasts and hips, fleshy thighs, a slightly broad ass. He saw nothing that he could complain about. She was a woman in her mid-thirties who had kept herself fit.

"I know what I look like," she told him, "so please, no lies. . . ."

He closed the gap between them and palmed her breasts.

"No lies," he said. "You're not a saloon girl, who has to keep herself thin to fit into a tight dress, and you're not a whore, who has to keep herself fit to stay in business. You're just a woman that any man would be proud to be with, as I am now. . . ."

"Jesus," she whispered, as if in awe, "no lies?"

He smiled and said, "No lies, Hailey."

He kissed her then, sliding his arms around her and cupping her buttocks in his hands, pulling her to him tightly. Her flesh was firm and hot, and she squirmed against him, sliding her hands down to cup his buttocks, as well.

"The bed," she said against his mouth, breathlessly.

He nodded and said, "The bed," and lowered her to it without removing the coverlet. . . .

SIXTEEN

They made love desperately, the desperation coming more from her than from him. Later, as they lay side by side on the still-made bed, she told him why.

"It's been a long time for me, Clint," she said, laying her hand on his belly as she spoke. "A long time since I've even *seen* a man I wanted, let alone been with one."

"It shouldn't have been so long, Hailey," he said. "You're a wonderful lover. You should have a man to be with all the time."

"Are you applying for the job?" she asked, then laughed shortly and said, "Never mind, you don't have to answer that. Don't worry. I know this for what it is."

"And what's that?"

"Just two people who knew they wanted this right from the first moment they met."

He remained silent.

"You . . . you did want me, didn't you?"

He laughed then and turned on his side, stroking her breasts with a feather light touch. Her nipples were

54

dark brown and large, and they responded quickly to his touch.

"Ink and all," he assured her.

She laughed and rolled into his arms. . . .

Later they pulled the coverlet down and slid beneath the sheets.

"I feel decadent," she said, stretching beneath the sheets.

"Why?" he asked.

"I should be working."

"Some time off never hurt anyone," he said.

She turned her head on the pillow, her hair fanned out around her, and she said, "You're not mad?"

"About the story?" he asked. "No."

"Why not?"

"Because I believe you," he said. "You weren't writing it to print in tomorrow's edition."

"Maybe not," she said, "but will I be able to use it in *any* edition?"

"Are you asking me if I intend to fight the Bonds?" he replied.

"I guess that's what I'm asking you."

"The answer is, I don't know," he said, "but I do have some questions about them."

"I'll answer them . . . if I can, but what do you say we get dressed first, and I'll make some coffee?"

"Sounds like a good idea," he agreed.

SEVENTEEN

"My questions are about the youngest one," Clint said over coffee. They were still upstairs, seated across her table from each other. She had excused herself for a moment to go downstairs and lock the front door.

"That'd be George."

"What do you know about him?"

"Just what I see."

"And what's that?"

"He's a pretty sick boy."

"Sick how?"

"Sick in the head, Clint."

"The kind who'd gut animals?" Clint asked. "Small animals?"

She nodded.

"Dogs and cats, mostly," she said. "Everybody in town knows about it, but they pretend not to. His *father* pretends not to."

"Is George dangerous?" Clint asked. "I mean, to anyone other than cats and dogs?"

"You mean to people," she said. "I've wondered

56

about that myself, from time to time. So far he's never shown any interest in people. I don't think he even likes girls."

"Boys?" Clint asked.

"He doesn't talk to people, Clint," she said. "It's as if they're not even there. I think that boy is in a world all his own."

"That sounds like the safest place for him," Clint said. "What about the daughter?"

"Now that's a real shame," she said.

"Why?"

"Because I've seen her, and she's real pretty," Hailey said. "I think she's a year or two younger than George. Clint, I can't imagine what it must have been like for a girl, growing up in that family."

"Pretty scary, I guess," he said. "Why doesn't she just leave?"

"She's probably afraid to," she said.

"I suppose," he said. "Tell me about the others. What've you noticed about them?"

"Well . . . Ben has a woman. He keeps her in her house, doesn't let her come out."

"Did he bring her here with him?"

"No," Hailey said, "he chose her when he got here. Her name's Meg Black. She used to have a store, women's clothing, but when Ben saw her and took to her, that was the end of her business."

"Did she sell it?"

"No," Hailey said, "it's just been closed all this time. He keeps her locked up in her own house, only he calls it *his* house, now."

"Two women, virtual prisoners of the Bonds," he said.

"And the town."

"Maybe," he said, "but the town could free itself, if it really wanted to."

"How?"

"Come on, Hailey," he said. "The townspeople could easily outnumber the Bonds if they banded together to drive them out."

"They'd need a leader, Clint," she said. "Someone to explain that to them."

"Do you think they'd listen?" he asked.

"I don't know," Hailey said. "Maybe that's something we should find out."

He stared across the table at her and said, "I'm still not sure I want to take a hand in this. I mean, why should I?"

"I don't know," she said. "Why should you?"

"No good reason I can think of."

"And tons of reasons why you shouldn't."

"Right."

"Right."

"I mean, why risk my neck for a bunch of people I don't even know?" he asked. "You're the only one I know in town."

"Me," Hailey said, "and Marcus Bond."

"I don't *know* him," he said. "I've just talked with him."

"And from that one conversation," she said, "I think you know him better than anyone who's lived in this town with him for the past year."

"Maybe," he said, "but that's only because I've known men like him before, men who love making other people afraid of them. I mean, that's how he gets what he wants, by scaring people."

"In this case," Hailey said, "an entire town to call his own."

Clint had been staring at his coffee, and now he looked across at her again.

"Are you afraid, Hailey?"

"Of Marcus Bond and his sons?"

He nodded.

"Damn right I am."

"Have you written about them at all?"

"I did, in the beginning," she said.

"What happened?"

"Marcus came to see me."

"And?"

"He told me that unpleasant things would happen to me if his name, or the names of any of his sons, showed up in my newspaper again."

"And?"

"And nothing," she said. "I didn't want to find out what those unpleasant things might be, so I never wrote about them again."

"Can't say I blame you much for that."

"I blame me, though."

"For what?"

"I probably could have used my newspaper to rouse the people, Clint. In the beginning, I mean, before the fear really set in."

"You can't blame yourself for what the townspeople do—or don't do."

"But I'm one of the townspeople," she said. "We *should* have banded together right there at the beginning and driven them out, but we didn't have a leader. We've never had anyone in town who might be a leader—until now."

She was staring right at him as she said it, and he shifted uncomfortably beneath her gaze.

"I have to get back to work," she said, standing

up. "Why don't you think it over and let me know what you decide to do? If you decide to leave town, I'll understand that."

She cleared the table of the cups and then turned to face him.

"My press will be on when you leave, so I won't hear you. Come back later, and we'll have dinner."

He stood up and said, "Maybe I'll use tonight to do some thinking, Hailey."

"Suit yourself," she said. "Tonight or tomorrow, I'll be here."

She turned and went down the stairs, leaving him alone with his thoughts.

Rather than remain in her home and struggle with himself, Clint decided to take a walk. True to her word, Hailey had the press going when he got downstairs, so she did not hear him leave.

Outside he began to wander aimlessly around the town, watching with interest the people he passed.

Damn it, he thought, if he didn't like the woman so much he probably *would* ride out of town and leave it to the Bonds. After all, what business was it of his? In the past he'd been drawn into other people's affairs so often that he had started trying to avoid it. Now here he was contemplating taking a hand on his own, with almost no urging from anyone else.

As he walked, the people he saw seemed content enough to be where they were. If anyone truly objected to Marcus Bond and his sons running the town, they were free to pack up and leave, weren't they?

Sure, he thought, tell them to just pack up and leave their homes. Rather than do that, they'd suffer the tyranny of a bully and his sons. Could he leave them to that? Could he leave Hailey Morgan to that? Or should he urge her to leave her old printing press behind and move on? And would she even consider that?

Clint decided to take his ruminations over to the saloon and wrestle with them over a beer . . . or two.

EIGHTEEN

It was just before dinnertime when Clint entered the saloon. The bartender recognized him and had a beer waiting on the bar by the time he reached it.

"That's what I call service," Clint said, taking the beer off the bar. "Thanks."

"Sure thing," the bartender said, and drifted away, wiping the bar and tossing sidelong glances at Clint. The man was either afraid of him, or respected him, probably because he had seen Marcus Bond and him together. Maybe it was because Clint had showed no fear when faced with Marcus Bond and his son, Ben. It might have been the first time the bartender had ever seen a man who was *not* afraid of them.

The saloon was busier than it had been earlier when Clint was there, but the same table he had taken before was still empty. He walked to it and sat with his beer, which he was in no hurry to finish. He just needed someplace to sit, and something to do while he was trying to make his decision, and this was as good a place as any.

Hailey Morgan didn't hear anyone come into her office. The press was far too noisy for that. No, rather

62

she *felt* the presence of someone, and when she turned around, she saw him standing there.

Sheriff Marcus Bond.

Sheriff, indeed, she thought. A self-appointed lawman was no lawman as far as she was concerned.

Bond pointed to the press, obviously wanting her to turn it off. She hesitated a moment, wishing she had the courage to ignore him, but in the end she walked to the press and turned it off.

"Sheriff," she said, when the man said nothing, "what can I do for you?"

"I understand you had a visitor earlier, Mrs. Morgan," Bond said.

"A visitor?"

"Clint Adams?" the man said. "He did come to see you, didn't he?"

"Oh, yes, Mr. Adams," Hailey said, nodding. Nervously, she dried her hands on the sides of her thighs. "Yes, he was here."

"Good," Bond said. She wasn't quite sure what he thought was good, that Clint had been there to see her, or that she was admitting to it. "Good," he said again, "we're gettin' somewhere."

"Are we?" she asked. "Where are we getting to, Sheriff?"

"I'd like to know what you and Clint Adams talked about, Mrs. Morgan," Bond said. "Would you tell me that, please?"

"He, uh, wanted to talk about the history of the town," she said.

"The town?"

"That's right."

Bond studied her for a moment, then said, "Are you sure he wasn't asking you about us?"

"Us?"

"Me and my sons."

"Well . . . as pertaining to the *history* of the town . . ." Hailey said, wishing that she had come up with a better lie. "I mean, he was just curious about the development of Allentown—"

"Allentown," Bond said, cutting her off. He looked away thoughtfully, then looked back at her. "You know, I've been thinking about changing the name of the town."

"Changing the name?"

"Yeah," Bond said, "Allentown doesn't appeal to me, anymore. What do you think of that, Mrs. Morgan . . . Hailey? Should we change the name of the town?"

"I don't think—"

"What did you tell Adams?" he asked, cutting her off again. "What did you tell him . . . about me?"

"Just that you were the sheriff."

"But not a duly *appointed* sheriff, right?" Bond asked. "I mean, you told him that, didn't you?"

"Well . . . yes, I did . . . but . . ."

"But what?"

"Well . . . I didn't see any reason *not* to tell him—I mean, about you and your sons—"

"*Taking* the jobs, you mean," Bond said. "About me taking the sheriff's job and naming my boys as deputies? You told him all of that?"

"Uh . . . yes, I did. . . ."

"I'll bet he found it very interesting," Bond said.

"Well—"

"Did he?"

"I, uh, don't—I can't say what he thought, Sheriff," she stammered.

"Then tell me what he said, Mrs. Morgan," he said,

then called her by her first name again. "Hailey . . .
tell me what he said."

"I . . . don't know—I mean, I'm not sure—"

She stopped short when the sheriff started to
approach her. She tensed as he got closer, and then
he was standing right in front of her.

"Hailey," he said. He reached out and stroked her
hair, which she had pinned back behind her head again.
"I need to know what Clint Adams is planning to
do . . . if anything. Can you tell me that?"

She opened her mouth to answer and found that she
couldn't make a sound. She realized with a shock that
she was truly frightened of this man, and that made
her suddenly angry.

"To tell you the truth, Sheriff," she said, "I don't
exactly know what Mr. Adams's plans are. You see,
he didn't confide in me. I told him what he wanted
to know, and then he left."

"You had lunch with him."

"Yes," she said, remembering that Red had seen
them. "I told him what he wanted to know over lunch,
and then I came back here."

"I see," Bond said. He reached out to touch her shoulders, and she felt herself cringe. He stopped just short
of touching her.

"Did you cringe that way," Bond asked, "when *he*
touched you?"

"Sheriff—"

Suddenly his hand came around and he slapped her
across the face. Her head rocked, her cheek stung, and
little spots of light flashed before her eyes.

"I'll ask you again, Hailey," she heard him say
from somewhere far away, "and this time I want the
truth. . . ."

NINETEEN

Clint was still working on the lone beer when a man approached his table.

"Are you Clint Adams?"

Clint looked the man up and down. He was tall and slender, gray-haired, maybe not yet fifty years old. He was well-dressed and did not look like a shopkeeper. Banker, Clint thought, or doctor—and probably a member of the town council.

"That's right."

"My name is Silas Moore," the man said, "Dr. Silas Moore. Do you mind if I sit down?"

"Suit yourself," Clint said.

A couple of girls had come to work about a half an hour earlier. They were both in their twenties and had probably been working in the saloon for some time. They seemed to know most of the customers and had an easy rapport with them.

Dr. Moore turned and motioned to one of the girls, who nodded and brought him a shot glass and a bottle of whiskey.

"Thank you, Rayanne," Silas Moore said. He poured

66

himself a shot, downed it, and poured another. That one he left on the table, sitting next to the bottle.

"What can I do for you, Doctor?" Clint asked.

"I've been wondering that myself, Mr. Adams," Moore said. "You see, word has gotten around town that you're here."

"Really?"

"Indeed," Moore said. "We've also heard that you had a conversation with our sheriff."

"Your self-appointed sheriff, you mean."

Moore smiled grimly and said, "Ah, that is my point."

"I thought it might be."

"What is your relationship with, uh, Sheriff Bond?" Moore asked.

"I don't have one," Clint said.

"I see," Moore said. "Then he was just . . . questioning you?"

"About my intentions regarding the town," Clint said, and then added, "as any good lawman would question a stranger."

"But Marcus Bond is not a good lawman, Mr. Adams," Moore said. "I mean, as we have already established, he is neither duly elected nor duly appointed."

"I know all of that."

"Then do you know that he and his sons have held this town beneath their thumb for the better part of a year?" Moore asked.

"Yes," Clint said, "I know that, too."

Moore stared at Clint and said, "You've been talking to someone."

Since Clint didn't know who Moore was—aside from who he *said* he was—and didn't know the man's relationship with Marcus Bond, he decided not to mention his conversations with Hailey Morgan at all.

"I pay attention, Doctor," he said instead.

"Mr. Adams, may I ask how long you intend to stay in town?"

"I haven't decided that yet, Doctor."

Clint finished his beer and set the empty mug on the table. The doctor turned immediately and motioned to Rayanne, who responded by coming to the table.

"Another beer for Mr. Adams, Rayanne," he said.

"Sure, Doc." She gave Clint a smile and went off to get the beer. She was a tall, big-breasted, long-legged brunette, and it was a pleasure to watch her whether she was coming or going.

"What do you expect to get for a beer, Doc?" Clint asked him.

"Perhaps a little bit more of your time, Mr. Adams," Moore said. "Could you spare me that?"

"Make your pitch."

"I—we—"

Clint held up his hand and said, "Before you make that pitch, Doc, I'd like to know who you're making it on behalf of."

"The town council has asked me to approach you," Moore said.

"This is the same town council that has allowed Marcus Bond and his sons to hold this town prisoner for a year?" Clint asked. "I mean, I'm just trying to get the full picture here, Doc."

"All right, yes, it is the same council," Moore said. "Mr. Adams, we have tried to hire men before to rid us of Marcus Bond and his crazy sons. We've never been able to get anyone."

"I doubt that you tried very hard, Doc," Clint said.

"How can you pass judgment on us when you've

only just arrived?" Dr. Moore asked.

"Like I told you, Doc," Clint said, "I pay attention."

At that point Rayanne came back with Clint's beer. She set it down in front of him while allowing her hips to brush his shoulder.

"Anything else?"

She was asking him, not the doctor.

"No," he said, "nothing else . . . right now."

"Just let me know," she said, and strolled away, her hips swaying provocatively.

"All right, Doctor," Clint said, "go ahead."

TWENTY

"We need your help," Silas Moore said.

"You've needed *somebody's* help for a long time, Doctor," Clint said.

"You are a very harsh judge, Mr. Adams."

"I just feel that people should try to help themselves, Doctor," Clint said, "and not rely on other people to do their dirty work for them. This town should have banded together long ago and gotten rid of Marcus Bond and his sons."

"I agree," Moore said. "Unfortunately, none of us had the courage to do that. I admit to that, myself. I am a coward."

"No, no," Clint said, waving that kind of talk away. "Now who's a harsh judge? You're not a coward, Doctor. Physically, you're unable to face up to men like Marcus Bond. That's not being a coward, that's facing reality. There's no point dying trying to do something you're incapable of doing, or trying to be something you're not able to be."

"Then you'll do it?" Dr. Moore asked.

"Do what?"

"Help us."

"In what way?"

"Why . . . getting rid of the Bonds."

"What exactly is it you want me to do, Doctor?" Clint asked. "Kill them?"

"Well . . ."

"I'm not a gun for hire."

"I . . . well, your reputation—"

"Forget about my reputation," Clint said, cutting the man off. "Listen to what I'm telling you. You can't hire my gun."

"Then . . . what *can* we hire you to do?" Moore asked.

"I'm not sure you can hire me to do anything," Clint said.

"Then you won't help us?"

"I didn't say that, either."

"I'm sorry, Mr. Adams," the doctor said, "but I'm more than a little confused."

"Well," Clint said, "that makes two of us, Doctor."

Hailey Morgan sat up and leaned against the printing press. She had thought that Marcus Bond was going to rape her. He tore her clothes, pawed her breasts, and she was sure that he was going to rape her. When he didn't do that, she became sure that he was going to kill her.

Throughout it all she had maintained that she did not know what Clint Adams's plans were. It was obvious to her that Marcus Bond was genuinely afraid of Clint. She had taken pleasure in that even as the man had been hitting her.

She tried to get up and gasped as pain lanced through her side, where Bond had punched her twice. She could also feel the bruises and swelling on her face, and she knew that her upper lip was split.

What she needed to do right now was get to the doctor—but before she could do that, she had to get up off the floor.

"I don't like what Marcus Bond is doing, Doctor," Clint said. "I've never liked men who make victims of other people."

"Well," Moore said, "he has certainly done that, he *and* his sons. Ben has virtually made a slave out of poor Meg Black." Moore shook his head. "You should have seen Meg Black a year ago, Mr. Adams. A beautiful woman, always smiling and laughing. No one has seen her in months. For all we know, she may even be dead."

Clint scowled. Moore seemed genuinely concerned for Meg Black and did not seem to be using her plight to persuade Clint, but that's what he was doing, even without realizing it. Clint hated men who victimized women.

"Tell me, please," Moore said, "how you've come to know so much about us."

Clint saw no harm now in speaking of Hailey. He was convinced that the doctor was who he said he was.

"I've spent some time with Hailey Morgan, Doctor," Clint said.

"Ah," Moore said, "our lovely newspaperwoman. You know, it's too bad some of the men in this town don't have her courage."

Clint didn't know what to say to that.

Moore pushed his chair back and stood up.

"I'll leave you to yourself, Mr. Adams," Moore said. "If you should decide that there *is* some way in which you can help us, will you let me know?"

"Yes, of course," Clint said.

"Then I thank you for your time, sir," Moore said and headed for the door.

The doctor was almost to the batwing doors when a young man entered, looking out of breath and distressed. He grabbed the doctor by the arm and spoke to him quickly. Moore said something to the young man, then quickly returned to Clint's table.

"You might want to come along with me," he said.

"Why?" Clint asked. "What's happened?"

"It seems Marcus Bond has beaten up Hailey Morgan."

TWENTY-ONE

Clint followed the doctor to his office, where they found Hailey Morgan waiting for them. Her face was battered, and from the way she was sitting hunched over, there were other injuries, as well.

"What happened?" Clint asked.

"I'm afraid your questions will have to wait until later," Dr. Moore said. "If you'll wait outside, I'll examine her."

"Was it Bond?" Clint asked her. "Marcus Bond?"

"Yes," she said through swollen lips.

"That's enough, Mr. Adams," Moore said. "Outside, please."

"I'll be back," Clint said.

"Clint—" Hailey called, but he was already out the door and on his way to the sheriff's office.

TWENTY-TWO

Marcus Bond sat in his office behind his desk with his sons around him. He knew that beating up Hailey Morgan had been a foolish thing to do. In fact, he hadn't gone there to do that, but once he'd started hitting her, he had found that he couldn't stop.

He liked it.

In fact, he liked it too much. It made him think of his son, George, with his small animals. Was that what George felt when he was gutting a small dog or a cat? Could it be that Bond was starting to understand his youngest son a little better now?

"Do you want to tell us what happened, Pa?" Ben asked.

What happened? He had tried to find out from Hailey Morgan what Clint Adams's plans were, and instead had ended up beating her. He knew that when Adams heard about that, he'd come after him.

Was that so bad?

Things might just work out for the best, yet.

"Pa?" Red said.

Ben and Red exchanged a glance while George was

staring off at something only he could see.

"Boys," Marcus Bond said finally, "we better get ready. I think maybe we're gonna have us a visitor pretty soon."

"Who, Pa?" Red asked.

Ben didn't have to ask. He knew who his father was talking about. He had seen the skinned knuckles on his father's hands when he walked back into his office, and Ben knew where his father had been. Ben had never known his father to beat a woman before, not even their mother or sister, but obviously that's what had happened between his father and Hailey Morgan. Now his father was figuring that Clint Adams would be coming after him for revenge.

"We'll be ready, Pa," he said.

Ben wondered if anything *else* had happened between his father and Hailey Morgan. Suddenly he had the urge to go to the house to be with Meg Black, but he'd wait until after his father finished talking.

Red Bond didn't know what was going on. He only knew that his father had changed, suddenly. There was something different about him when he came back from talking to that newspaper lady.

Red looked at his brother for some explanation, but Ben just looked away. Red's older brother had a funny look on his face, too.

As for George, Red knew his younger brother was in his own little world. Inside his head he was probably skinning some kind of an animal. Red shuddered. George scared the hell out of him. He respected his father, and Ben as well, but George was the one he was genuinely *afraid* of.

• • •

"How did the two of you come to be together when you heard about me?" Hailey asked Silas Moore.

"Quiet," Moore said. "I want to check your teeth and jaw. Just move it when I move it."

She stared at him, repeating her question with her eyes.

"I went to talk to him," Moore finally said.

"About what?"

"Can't you stop talking?" he said. "Jesus, just like a woman—and a newspaperwoman, to boot."

Hailey knew that Doc Moore was sweet on her, and for the most part he was a decent man, but he didn't have the backbone God gave a jellyfish. Decent men were fine, but she needed a decent man who also had some spine—like Clint Adams.

"I wanted to ask him for his help," Moore said, while probing her jaw. "I tried to hire him."

"What did he—"

"Quiet, Hailey!" Moore snapped. "He said his gun wasn't for hire, and that he didn't know if he was interested in trying to help us. He also said he had spent some time talking to you."

"So?"

"Nothing," Moore said, moving back from her and looking at her critically. "Your jaw isn't broken. You have a couple of loose teeth, but I don't think you'll lose them. You might have a broken rib, but then again it might just be bruised. Only time will tell. All in all, you could be in a lot worse shape."

She probed her upper lip with her tongue and flinched at the pain.

"You won't be kissing anyone for a while with that lip," Moore said.

"Ha," she said and flinched again.

"So . . . what did you and Mr. Adams talk about?" Moore asked, trying to seem unconcerned.

She eased herself down from his examining table and said, "The same thing you talked to him about."

She started to button her shirt and tuck it into her pants. Her breasts had bruise marks on them from Marcus Bond's fingers.

Moore shook his head and, without looking at her, said, "Oh, I doubt that."

"Do you have something else you want to ask me, Silas?" Hailey asked.

Moore did, but he didn't have the nerve to ask her if she had slept with Clint Adams.

"No, Hailey," he said. "We're done. Just take it easy for a while. Why the hell was Bond hitting you, anyway?"

She hesitated a moment, then said, "In the beginning he was trying to get me to tell him about Clint."

"And in the end?"

"In the end," she said, "I think he just started to like it."

When Hailey stepped out of Silas Moore's office she found Clint Adams waiting for her.

"You're here," she said.

"Of course I'm here."

"I thought . . ."

"What?" he asked, taking her arm. "That I'd go after Bond?"

She nodded.

"I did, but I stopped myself. There's no point in getting myself killed because I'm angry."

"Good," she said. "I'm glad you didn't."

"Come on," he said, "I'll take you home, and we'll talk—or rather, I'll talk and you'll listen close."

"Does that mean you're going to stay awhile?" she asked.

"It means," he said, "we have some planning to do."

TWENTY-THREE

Clint took Hailey back home and made sure he locked the door to her office before they went upstairs.

"I don't want to go to bed," she said when they reached there. Then she looked at him slyly and added, "Unless you come with me."

"Feeling up to that, are you?" he asked.

"Actually," she said sadly, "no."

"Well," he said, "if the doctor says you might have a broken rib, bed is the best place for you. There's nothing you can do for that but wait for it to heal."

"I don't think I have a broken rib," she said. "It doesn't hurt *that* much."

"Does it hurt when you breathe?" he asked.

She took a deep breath and then said, "No, only when I move a certain way."

"If it was a cracked rib, it would hurt just to breathe," he said.

"There, see? I'm not going to bed."

"Well then, sit down. I'll make some coffee."

"You'll make coffee?"

"I *can* make coffee, you know."

"Good coffee?" she asked.

"Well," he said, hedging, "trail coffee. It's not quite the same thing. On the trail I just need something strong and hot, I'm not so concerned with actual taste."

"Ugh," she said, "I think I'm going to regret this."

Clint put the coffeepot on the stove and got it going, and then sat opposite Hailey at the table.

"Okay," he said, "tell me what happened."

She shuddered, and he reached out and took both of her hands in his while she told him the story. . . .

"I thought he was going to kill me," she finished. "First I thought he was going to rape me, and then I thought he was going to kill me. And you know what? I don't know which would have been worse."

Her hands had gone ice-cold, and he held them tightly in a futile effort to warm them.

"It's all right," he said, and it sounded inane even to him.

"I want to kill him," she said quietly. "He frightened me. I'll be frightened now for a long time because of what he did, and I want to kill him."

"I know," Clint said, "I know, but that's not the way to do it."

"What is, then?" she asked.

"The fear."

"What about it?"

"These men," Clint said, "men like Marcus Bond, they rule by fear. If you take the fear away from them, the fear as a *weapon*, then they have nothing."

"And how do you do that?" she asked. "I mean, sure, I was afraid of them before, but this fear—what I feel now—is totally different. I can understand now how someone can be too scared to move!"

Clint smiled and said, "You and I are going to get this town to finally stand up to them."

"How, Clint?" Hailey asked. "How do we do that?"

"I don't know yet, Hailey," he said. "What I do know is men like Marcus Bond. That's an advantage to us."

"And what about Marcus Bond?" she asked. "What does he know?"

"He knows what he's like," Clint said, "and he expects everyone else to be like that, too. It's the only way he knows."

She stared at Clint and said, "It's as if you've known men like him all your life."

"I've known all kinds of men, Hailey," Clint said. "I've known good men, bad men, weak men, strong men, but men aren't always just one way. I mean, it's not all black-and-white, there are plenty of different shades of gray in between."

"And Marcus Bond?"

"Not only Marcus Bond," Clint said, "but all of the Bonds, they're right smack in the black. Marcus and Ben abuse women; George *definitely* has something black inside of him to be able to do what he does to small animals. I mean, left alone how long would it be before he moved on to people?"

"And Red?"

"I don't have a handle on Red," Clint said. "Possibly he just goes along with the others. We'll find that out, too, because we might be able to use him. While the others are black, he might fall into a shade of gray— *weak* and gray."

"My God," she said suddenly.

"What?"

She pulled her hands from his.

"I should be taking notes," she said. "This will all make a *wonderful* story when it's all over."

She stood up—too fast, wincing—and went off to find a pencil and paper.

Clint smiled as he watched her. It was a demonstration of not only her strength but of her courage that she was not so frightened that she forgot she was a newspaperwoman.

He stood up and poured two cups of coffee. He wondered if she'd be brave enough to drink it.

TWENTY-FOUR

Ben looked out the window again, then turned to face his father. Red was standing by the stove, drinking coffee. George—well, George was in the room, but there was no telling *where* he really was.

"Where is he?" Ben asked.

"I don't know," Marcus said, frowning. "He should have been here by now."

"Maybe he won't come after you, Pa," Red said.

"Of course he will, Red," Marcus said. "Jesus Christ, I beat up his lady friend. Any man would come after me after that."

"Any man who's a man," Ben said. "Maybe he can't live up to his reputation. Maybe I should go and find him and find out."

"No," Marcus said, "not yet. You'll get your chance, Ben, but not yet."

"Why not, Pa?"

"Because we got to find out what we're dealin' with, here."

"A man, Pa," Ben said. "We're dealin' with a man who won't stand up for his woman."

"No," Marcus said, "there's somethin' else goin' on here."

"Like what?" Red asked.

"I don't know!" Marcus snapped in frustration. "But somethin'."

"Pa—" Ben started, but Marcus waved him silent with a vicious chop at the air.

Marcus Bond couldn't understand what was happening. If someone had beaten up *his* woman, he would have gone after him right away. What was keeping Clint Adams? Why hadn't he come? If he had, it would all be over by now. They'd be lowering Adams's body into an unmarked grave tomorrow.

"Pa," Ben said, "I'm goin' out."

"Go ahead," Marcus said, "but stay away from Adams. You hear me, boy?"

"I hear you, Pa," Ben said and went outside.

The old man is afraid, Ben thought on the boardwalk in front of the office. He's afraid of Clint Adams's reputation. Well, the oldest son thought, he may be afraid, but I'm not.

Even though Ben felt superior to his father now, he still respected him. He was told not to go after Adams, and he wasn't going to.

Not yet, anyway.

He turned and started walking south, toward Meg Black's house.

After Ben left, George started for the door without saying a word. Marcus looked up and watched his youngest son go out the door. He knew he didn't have to warn George to stay away from Clint Adams. He also knew that if he sent George after Adams, his youngest boy would go without a question, without even a word. George might be a strange one, but he did what his father told him. Ben was getting to the point, Marcus knew, when he was going to try to test his strength against his father's. Marcus knew he was going to have to be ready for that.

"You want me to stick around, Pa?" Red asked.

Marcus looked at Red, who was neither as strong as Ben nor as unquestioning as George.

"No, Red," Marcus said. "Why don't you go and do some rounds? I don't think Clint Adams is comin' today."

"Okay, Pa," Red said. "I'll be around if you need me."

"Sure, Red," Marcus said. He barely looked up as Red went out the door.

Outside Red saw George walking down the street. What else are you gonna skin today, little brother? he found himself thinking. He wondered if George would ever get tired of killing small animals and start in on people. What would Pa do then? he wondered. Could he ignore that?

Red shuddered. He knew *he* couldn't ignore it. If that ever happened he was leaving, going off on his own . . . only where would he go? What would he do without his father to tell him what to do?

Oddly, he thought about his sister then. Nancy was smart, smarter than him or Ben. She was definitely smarter than George. Red didn't know if she was smarter than his father, but he knew she wasn't happy here in Allentown. Maybe she'd want to leave, too. Maybe *she* could tell him what to do.

He turned north and started walking toward his father's house, where Nancy was.

• • •

Marcus knew that he and his boys had had it easy here for the past year. They'd never had to face anyone like Clint Adams, though. Adams was obviously not like any other man. Anyone else would have come charging after Marcus after he found out what had happened to Hailey Morgan. For Adams *not* to do that confused Marcus Bond to the point where he wasn't sure what to do about it now.

Marcus Bond didn't like not knowing what to do.

TWENTY-FIVE

Hailey finally succumbed to Clint's urgings, to the bruises and the pain, *and* to Clint's coffee. She allowed Clint to put her into bed.

"Will you be here when I wake up?" she asked.

"I'm going out," he said, "but only for a minute. I'll be right back."

"I want you to stay here," she said sleepily.

"I'll be back."

"No, Clint," she said, "I mean *stay* here, not at the hotel."

"Hailey—"

"I'm scared."

"All right," he said, "I'll collect my gear and stay here."

She smiled, said, "Good," and fell fast asleep.

He left her there, went down to the office, and let himself out. He was worried about leaving her alone, even for a little while, but he felt sure that Marcus Bond and his boys would be waiting now to see what he was going to do. He had some time, then, before they decided to come after him.

Walking to the doctor's office, he went over it in his

mind. His intention—as things stood right now—was to try to get the town to go against the Bonds. Hopefully, he'd be able to do that before the Bonds came after him. If they did come after him, he was going to have to defend himself. But if he got rid of the Bonds, the town of Allentown would have learned nothing. The townspeople needed to rid *themselves* of Marcus Bond and his sons.

He entered the doctor's office. From the small waiting room he could hear voices in the examination room. He sat down to wait, but he'd wait only a short time. He had to get to the hotel to collect his gear and then get back to Hailey Morgan's.

He was there five or six minutes and was about to leave when the door to the examination room opened and Dr. Moore came out leading a small boy and his mother. The boy's hand was wrapped.

"He should be fine, Mrs. O'Brien," Dr. Moore was saying. "Just keep it clean, and it will heal quickly."

"Thank you, Doctor."

Moore showed the woman and boy to the door, then turned to face Clint.

"Mr. Adams."

Clint stood up.

"Get your town council together, Doc," Clint said. "I want to talk to them."

"You'll help us?" Moore asked.

"No," Clint said, "but I'll help you help yourselves. That's my best offer. Take it or leave it."

Moore didn't hesitate.

"We'll take it, Mr. Adams," Moore said. "How much will it cost us?"

"Just get them together as soon as you can and let me know when you'll meet," Clint said.

"You'll be at the hotel?"

"I'm staying at Mrs. Morgan's," Clint said.

"Hailey's?"

Clint studied the doctor for a few moments. When they first met, the man's gray hair had fooled him. Clint now believed that instead of being close to fifty, the doctor was probably younger than he was. He was also sure that the man had feelings for Hailey Morgan.

"Marcus Bond might go after her again, Doctor," Clint said. "We wouldn't want that, would we?"

"No," Moore said quietly. "No, we wouldn't."

"Let me know when you and your colleagues are ready, Doctor," Clint said.

"I'll do that, Mr. Adams," Moore said. "Thank you."

Clint nodded and left. Was there going to be a problem between him and the doctor over Hailey now? He hoped not. He certainly didn't need that kind of problem on top of everything else.

After Clint left the doctor's office, Silas Moore sat down in his own waiting room. He'd probably be able to convene a meeting of the council by morning if he left now and spoke to each of them. There were five others who sat on the council with him, and they all ran businesses in town.

He remembered the meeting they'd had when Marcus Bond had first announced that he was now the sheriff of Allentown.

"What do we do about it?" Sam Carlisle had asked. Carlisle ran the general store.

"What *can* we do?" Will Cord said. Will owned the feed and grain, the livery stable, and a saddle shop. "We do need a sheriff."

"Not Marcus Bond," Moore had said. "Not a self-appointed sheriff."

"So what do we do?" Tom Stamp asked. Stamp was the bank manager. "Tell him to leave?"

"Ha, yeah," Kevin Riley said. Riley owned the hardware store. "*You* tell him to leave."

Moore turned and looked at the sixth member of the council.

"Judge?"

Judge Eric Bishop looked at each member of the council in turn.

"Are any of you willing to tell the man he has to leave?" he asked.

There was some grumbling, but no one was willing to volunteer.

"That's what I thought," Bishop said. "Gentlemen, I think we have a new sheriff."

TWENTY-SIX

Clint checked out of the hotel and carried his gear to Hailey Morgan's office. He entered and locked the door behind him. He looked around. The office seemed totally different when it was quiet. He walked to the press and put his hand on it. The edition she was working on would now probably never get out on time—whenever that was. He leaned over to look at one of the sheets. It was the front page, and it had tomorrow's date on it.

He picked up his gear and walked upstairs. Setting his belongings down on the floor, he poured himself another cup of coffee and sat at the table with it. He sipped it a few times, then got up and looked out the back window. There was an alleyway down below. He walked into the front room, careful not to wake Hailey, and looked out the front window, which overlooked the main street. Satisfied, he went back to the table and sat.

Would Marcus Bond come after Hailey Morgan again? Initially he had gone to her for information on Clint. Whatever reason he had for starting to hit her, if she read the situation right, he had just gone crazy. There was no real reason for him to have beaten her, except that he had found himself enjoying it. Given time to think about it, why would Bond come after her again? It didn't make any sense. Still, as long as Hailey was afraid, he'd stay with her. Knowing her—and he *had* come to know her in the short time since he'd met her—he figured the fear wouldn't last very long.

Besides, she'd get tired of his coffee pretty quick.

When the front door opened, Nancy Bond held her breath and walked out of the kitchen to see which of her relatives was home. When she saw that it was Red, she released the breath. Of her father and brothers, Red was the only one she wasn't afraid of.

"Red," she said. "What's wrong?"

Red walked to the sofa and sat down.

"I don't know what to do."

"About what?" she asked.

"Clint Adams."

"Who's Clint Adams?"

Red looked up at his sister and then hurriedly explained the situation to her.

"Why did Pa beat up Miz Morgan?"

"I don't know, Nancy," Red said. "I think he just . . . liked it."

Nancy shuddered. Under normal circumstances her father scared her, but she had never seen him beat her mother, and he had never hit her. If he suddenly started *enjoying* hitting a woman . . .

"I don't know what to do, Nancy," Red complained.

"We could leave, Red," she said, seizing the opportunity she had been waiting a long time for.

"Leave Pa?" he asked. Red had thought about it, but he had never said or heard the words aloud.

Nancy sat next to her brother on the sofa.

"He doesn't need us, Red," she said. "He has Ben and George. You and me, we're a big disappointment to Pa. Me because I'm not Ma, and you . . ."

"I know," Red said, "me because I'm not smart like Ben, or strong like Pa, or . . ."

"We can leave, Red," she said, putting her hand on the back of his neck.

He looked at his sister and said, "You been wantin' to leave for a long time, ain't you?"

"Yes," she said, "a very long time."

She watched her brother hopefully. Would he agree? Would she finally have someone to take her away from here? She held her breath and waited.

"I got to think about it, Nancy," Red finally said.

"Sure you do, Red," she said. "It's a big decision to make."

"I don't know what I'd do without Pa."

"Don't worry, Red," she said, rubbing his neck. "I'll take care of you, and you'll take care of me. We'll watch out for each other, the way a brother and sister should."

"I suppose . . ." Red said. He looked at her then and asked, "We got anything to eat?"

"Sure," she said. "I'll get dinner ready."

She went into the kitchen and started dinner. She was shocked a few moments later to find that she was humming to herself.

In the living room Red was even more confused than ever. Even though he'd been thinking about leaving, to have actually *talked* about it made him nervous. What if Pa found out? What if Nancy told him? Should he tell Pa that Nancy had mentioned it, so that Pa wouldn't get mad at him?

Nancy had said they should act like a real brother and sister. Red Bond wasn't sure he even knew what that meant.

TWENTY-SEVEN

Clint got into bed with Hailey that night without waking her, and got up the same way the next morning. She was sleeping so soundly that he had taken a moment to lean over her and make sure she was all right. Maybe, in addition to the beating and the scare Marcus Bond had given her, she had simply *needed* to get some rest.

He made a fresh pot of coffee and then thought he heard someone knocking on the office door downstairs. He pulled on his pants and went down to see who it was.

The face in the window was young and familiar to him. When he opened the door, he realized that it was the same young man who had come to the saloon yesterday to fetch the doctor for Hailey.

"Good morning," Clint said.

"Uh, Mr. Adams?" the young man asked. He looked to be about nineteen years old.

"That's right."

"Doc Moore sent me over, sir," the kid said.

"What's your name, son?"

"Carl, sir."

"Carl what?"

"Wilkes."

"What's the message, Carl?"

"Oh, he says to tell you that the council will be meeting at nine a.m. in the town hall."

"Where's the town hall, Carl?" Clint asked.

"Down the street, sir, past the sheriff's office but before the saloon."

"Big brick building?"

"That's right."

"Okay," Clint said, "you tell the doctor I'll be there."

"Yes, sir, I'll tell him."

Clint wondered if he should give the young man some money, but then decided that Carl was too old to be given two bits for delivering a message.

After Carl left, Clint closed the door, locked it, and went back upstairs.

"Clint?" Hailey called from the bed.

Clint went into the room.

"How do you feel?"

She shifted in the bed and winced.

"Stiff," she said.

"Yeah, you'll be stiff for a while."

"The voice of experience?" she asked.

He smiled.

"I've had my share of beatings over the years," he admitted.

She ran her hands over her face and pushed her hair back.

"I must look a fright."

"No worse than you did when we first met."

She looked at him and said, "Oh, thanks."

"You want some coffee?"

"Did you make it?"

"Of course."

She made a face, then said, "Well, maybe one cup to help me wake up."

Clint brought the coffee over, sat on the bed, and handed the cup to her.

"Did you spend the night here?" she asked.

"Yep."

"In bed with me?"

"Yes."

"I must have slept like a rock."

"You did," Clint said. "I think you must have needed it, even before Marcus Bond visited you."

"Visited," she said, and then shuddered as a chill swept over her.

"I'm sorry," he said.

"It's all right," she said. "It's just that, for a moment, I forgot. . . ."

"I have to go out this morning," Clint said.

"Where?"

"The town hall," he said. "The council is meeting, and I want to be there."

"Do you have to?"

"Well," he said, "I kind of called the meeting."

"Of course," she said.

"You could come with me, if you like."

"Because I'm scared to be alone?" she asked.

"Because you run a newspaper."

"That's right," she said, suddenly excited. "This will be news."

"It might."

"When is the meeting?"

"In half an hour."

"I've got to get ready," she said. She tossed the sheet back and started to get up, but her bruises protested and she moaned.

"Better go slow," he said. "They'll wait for us."

"They'd better," she said, easing her feet to the floor.

"They have to," Clint said. "Without me there's no meeting, and no news."

"That's true."

He walked over to pour some water into a basin for her, then she began to wash herself. She studied herself in a mirror for a moment and said, "Oh, shit," beneath her breath.

She took off her nightshirt, and he could see that her left side was bruised. She was totally unself-conscious of her nakedness. When she turned to dry herself, he saw that her breasts had finger bruise marks on them. Other than that, they were lovely.

"What are you going to tell them?"

"I haven't decided yet," he said. "All I know is I've got to make them realize that getting rid of Marcus Bond is their responsibility, not mine or anyone else's."

She needed help getting her jeans on, and he was glad to oblige.

As he touched her bare thighs she said, "Ooh, if I wasn't half dead . . ."

"Later," he said, pulling her pants up for her so she could button them.

She ran a brush through her hair, then turned and asked, "How do I look?"

Her upper lip was still split, but the swelling had gone down. Her right cheek had a livid bruise, and her lip had scabbed over.

"You look great," he told her.

"You've got to learn to lie better," she said. She looked around, picked up her notebook, and said, "I'm ready."

"Let's do it, then."

TWENTY-EIGHT

On the way to the town hall, Hailey briefed Clint on the members of the council.

As they reached the hall, Clint recited it back to her.

"Sam Carlisle, general store," he said. "He's hard-nosed, right?"

"Right," she said. "He'd be your best bet to appeal to. He wanted to do something in the beginning; he just didn't know how."

"Will Cord," Clint said, "feed and grain, livery. He was willing to accept Bond as sheriff."

"He figured one sheriff was as good as another," Hailey said.

"Tom Stamp's the bank manager," Clint said.

"He's the one to talk to if you're concerned about money," she said.

"I'm not."

"Clint, these men might accept what you say more readily if you make them pay for it."

"I'll keep that in mind," he said. "Let's see . . . Kevin Riley . . . the hardware store, right?"

"Right," she said. "Kevin's the youngest of the group, and he fancies himself a ladies' man."

"And then there's the judge," Clint said, "Judge Eric Bishop."

"The judge has been here for years and years, Clint," Hailey said. "He's a sensible man. At the time, it seemed sensible to him just to accept Marcus Bond and his sons. When he realized that it wasn't so sensible, it was too late."

"It's never too late to right a wrong, Hailey," Clint said.

"Ooh," she said as they reached the door, "can I quote you?"

Inside Dr. Silas Moore and his fellow council members waited impatiently.

"Well, is he gonna do it, or what?" Sam Carlisle demanded.

"I told you, Sam," Moore replied, "I don't know *what* he's going to do."

"But he has agreed to work for us, right, Silas?" Tom Stamp asked.

Moore looked at the banker.

"No, Tom, he hasn't."

"Then what the hell are we doin' here?" Kevin Riley asked.

"We're here because he asked to speak to all of us at one time," Moore explained. "After he does that, I guess he'll make up his mind one way or the other."

"One of *us* probably should have talked to him, instead of Silas," Cord said.

"Hey," Moore said, spreading his hands, "any of you could have stepped up and volunteered. I didn't see any of you doing so."

"Silas is right," the judge said, coming to his defense. "He's the only one who was willing to talk to Mr. Adams."

"Hell," Kevin Riley said, "for all we know, him and Marcus Bond are buddies."

"Do you have anything to back that up, Kevin?" the judge asked.

"We all know Adams's reputation," Riley said, looking around for support. "The man is a killer. Hell, he might even be worse than Marcus Bond and his sons. Did you ever think of that?"

"If he's gonna do us any good," Tom Stamp said, "he better be."

Moore was about to say something, but the door opened, admitting Clint Adams and Hailey Morgan, and all conversation stopped.

TWENTY-NINE

The council members all got to their feet.

"What's she doin' here?" Kevin Riley demanded.

Stamp shot him a sharp look. They could all see her bruised face.

"Mrs. Morgan is here at my request," Clint answered.

"With all due respect, I don't think—" Will Cord started, but he was cut off by the judge.

"I don't see any reason why Mrs. Morgan can't stay," he said. "Mr. Adams? I'm Judge Eric Bishop."

"Good to meet you, Judge," Clint said.

"I'll introduce you around the table," the judge said, and named Carlisle, Stamp, Cord, and Riley in turn. "You already know Dr. Moore."

"Yes."

"Well, Mr. Adams," Judge Bishop said, "we're all here, as you requested."

"But not for long," Kevin Riley said. "I've got work to do."

"You're free to leave now, if you like, Mr. Riley," Clint said. "I sure don't want to keep anyone here against their will."

Riley stared at Clint, then looked around the table and found that everyone in the room was looking at him.

"Uh, no . . . no, I'll stay," he stammered.

"Fine," Clint said. "May we sit?"

"Please," the judge said, and both Clint and Hailey sat down at the table, followed by the council members.

"Mrs. Morgan, we heard what happened to you at the hands of Marcus Bond," the judge said. "I, for one, regret it and feel partly responsible."

"Judge?" she said, frowning.

"If we had taken steps to get rid of Marcus Bond a long time ago, it never would have happened."

"That's true," Clint said, before Hailey had a chance to answer, "but maybe it's not too late to take those steps."

"That's what we're trying to do," Tom Stamp said, "by hiring you."

"No," Clint said, "I've already explained to Dr. Moore that I am not a gun for hire."

"That's not what your reputation indicates," Kevin Riley said.

"Maybe not," Clint said, "but I'm stating fact. My gun is not for hire."

"Then what are we doin' here?" Riley demanded.

"We're here to discuss what you can do to rid your town of Marcus Bond and his sons," Clint said.

"With or without your help?" the judge asked.

"With."

"You just finished saying—" Sam Carlisle started, but Clint finished for him.

"That I wasn't for hire," Clint said. "If I help you, it will be for free."

"Nothing's for free," Tom Stamp said.

"You're the banker, right?" Clint asked.

"That's right."

"I won't want any money for myself," Clint said, "but there may be a price. I propose that we discuss it later—*after* Marcus Bond is gone."

"That's sort of like asking us to sign a blank check," Stamp said.

"I have to agree with Tom," the judge said. "Can't you give us an idea of what the price might be?"

"No," Clint said, "all I can say is I won't ask for anything you can't pay."

"That's still leaves a lot of latitude," Stamp said.

"You'll have to discuss it, I know," Clint said, "but don't take too long."

"So," Sam Carlisle said, "what is it you are offering us, exactly?"

"My help."

"To do what?"

"To get your town ready to stand up to Marcus Bond and his sons."

"You mean," Carlisle asked, "for us to do it ourselves?"

"That's right," Clint said, "as you should have in the very beginning."

"If we wanted to do that," Riley said, "we wouldn't need you."

"Ah, but you do," Clint said. "Without me, I don't see any of you even getting out of your chairs."

Riley looked at the rest of the men at the table and said, "I don't like it. He's not offering to *do* anything for us."

"Perhaps not," the judge said, "but perhaps he *shouldn't* do anything *for* us."

"What do you mean, Judge?" Stamp asked.

"Maybe it's time we did something for ourselves," Judge Bishop said.

The judge looked at Clint, who smiled and said, "Good call, Judge."

Clint stood up, and Hailey with him.

"You gentlemen will want to discuss this," Clint said. "I'll be having breakfast with Mrs. Morgan."

"About Mrs. Morgan," the judge said.

"Yes?" Hailey said.

"Will any of this be showing up in the newspaper any time soon?" he asked.

"That would be like telling Marcus Bond what you're planning to do," she said. "No, I've agreed with Mr. Adams that I won't write anything until after the fact. That way everyone will be able to read how we stood up to the Bonds and chased them from our town."

"We don't want to chase them," Carlisle said. "We want to kill them."

"There's an attitude you're much too late in voicing," Clint said. "Think it over, gentlemen. Dr. Moore can tell me what your decision is. If you agree to take on what is essentially your own responsibility, we'll meet again."

"And if we don't agree?" Riley asked.

Clint looked at Kevin Riley and said, "I'll ride out of town, and you'll be back where you started."

THIRTY

The discussion began in earnest as soon as Clint was out the door, with most of them trying to talk at once.

"Order!" Judge Bishop shouted, slapping the palm of his hand down on the table.

Riley looked at Bishop and said, "We're not in your court, Judge."

"And you're damned lucky you're not," Bishop said. "All right, Kevin. You seem to have the most to say. Go ahead."

"We don't need this Adams to tell us what to do," Riley said. "He's not offerin' anything, and who knows what he's gonna ask for as payment?"

"I take it you vote no, then?" the judge asked.

"Are we puttin' it to a vote now?" Riley asked.

Bishop looked around the room, and when no one objected he said, "Yes, we are."

"Then I vote no."

"Fine," Bishop said. "Tom?"

Tom Stamp said, "I think I should have a one-on-one talk with Mr. Adams before we agree to anything."

"To what purpose?"

"I'm going to offer him money—a lot of money—to take care of the Bonds for us. His way sounds too dangerous, and it sounds as if it will take too long."

"Whose money will you be offering him, Tom?" Carlisle asked.

"My own."

"No," Will Cord said, "if he agrees, I'll kick in."

"He won't agree," Silas Moore said.

"There's no harm in trying," Stamp said.

"And if that doesn't work?" the judge asked. "What will your vote be?"

"If he doesn't accept the money?" Stamp said. "I'll vote yes."

The judge looked at Will Cord.

"Will?"

"Yes," Cord said, "either way."

"Silas, I think we know what you vote."

"I vote yes," Moore said, nodding.

"Sam?"

"I vote yes right now."

"So do I," the judge said. He looked at Riley and asked, "Kevin, do you want to change your vote?"

"No," Riley said, standing up. "I think we're makin' a mistake." With that he left hurriedly.

"Why don't I trust him?" Sam Carlisle asked the table at large.

"You think he'll go to Bond?" the judge asked.

"I'd hate to think that," Tom Stamp said.

"He never did fight very hard against Bond, did he?" Will Cord asked.

"Well," Stamp said, "that will soon be Clint Adams's problem, won't it? One way or another."

• • •

Outside Clint said to Hailey, "What do you think about Riley?"

"I've never liked him," she said.

"Do you think he'll go to Bond with any of this?" he asked.

"Oh," she said, thinking hard, "I'm not sure, Clint. You think he will?"

"I don't know him that well."

"You know him well enough to ask the question."

"And maybe well enough to wait out here for him and see where he goes when the meeting is over?"

She smiled and said, "Good idea."

Clint told Hailey to go to the café and wait for him. He'd be along soon. After she had gone, he took up a position across the street to wait for Kevin Riley.

He only had to wait about ten minutes for Riley to appear. He came out the front door, looked up and down the street, then started north, in the direction of both the hardware store and the sheriff's office.

Clint followed him across the street. The man was not moving quickly, but he was walking purposefully. If Clint had to bet at that moment, he would have put his money on Riley stopping at the sheriff's office.

They reached the office soon enough, and when Riley slowed, Clint thought he'd won his bet with himself. However, the man picked up speed again and walked past the office. Once he was past he increased his speed, as if he wanted to get as far away from the office as he could before he changed his mind.

Obviously, the man had thought about stopping and had then decided against it. That didn't mean that he wouldn't eventually go to Bond, anyway.

Clint followed him the rest of the way to the hardware store and when the man went inside, he changed his direction and headed for the café, and breakfast with Hailey.

He thought that Riley was the only real opposition to his proposal. The others would probably outvote him. Stamp, being the money man, would probably offer him money before they actually accepted his proposal, but in the end he thought that they would accept. What he had to do now was come up with some sort of a plan, something the people of the town would believe in.

Even when ten men are facing one, if every one of those ten men is afraid to die and doesn't want to be the first to get shot, that one man would be able to bully them. Clint was going to have to convince all ten that they could easily overpower the one.

THIRTY-ONE

Clint joined Hailey at the café for breakfast, and they were just being served when Tom Stamp, the banker, came walking in.

"I thought I might find you here," Stamp said. "I know Hailey likes to eat here."

"Hello, Tom," Hailey said.

"Hailey," Stamp said, nodding. "Mr. Adams, may I speak with you?"

"Sure," Clint said, "if you don't mind me eating while you talk."

"No, of course not," Stamp said. "I'm sorry to interfere with your breakfast."

"Take a seat," Clint said. "Have a cup of coffee."

"Uh," Stamp said, looking uncertain, "do you think we could, um, speak in private?"

"You can say whatever you want to say in front of Mrs. Morgan," Clint said.

Stamp gave Hailey a worried look.

"I won't take any notes, Tom," she said, holding up her right hand. "I promise."

"Well . . . all right," Stamp said, pulling another chair over.

"Coffee?" Clint offered again.

"No, thanks."

"Then what's on your mind?"

"I'd like to offer you five thousand dollars to take care of this . . . Marcus Bond matter for us," Stamp said, watching Clint carefully for his reaction. He flicked his eyes to Hailey once, but then looked back at Clint.

Clint put down his fork, picked up his coffee cup and took a sip, then set it down carefully. He did not pick up his fork again.

"Mr. Stamp," Clint said, "I know you were at the meeting this morning because I saw you. Weren't you listening?"

"Of course I was listening—"

"I said I wasn't for hire," Clint said. "Do you recall that?"

"Yes, I do," Tom Stamp said, "but I naturally assumed you meant not for *wages*. I mean, five thousand dollars is a lot of money—"

"Yes, it is," Clint said, "but what I said still stands. My gun is not for hire."

"What if I offered more—"

"No," Clint said sharply. "No, Mr. Stamp, you're *not* listening."

"I *am* listening—" Stamp insisted.

"Then you obviously just don't understand me."

"No, I don't," Stamp said. "I'm prepared to offer *ten* thousand dollars. How can a man with your reputation say no to that?"

"I have said no, Mr. Stamp," Clint said, "and now I'd like to eat my breakfast."

Clint sat there staring at Stamp until the man got the message and stood up.

"I'm, uh, sorry if I've offended you, Mr. Adams," the banker stammered.

"You have," Clint said.

"Well . . . I'm sorry. . . ."

When Clint didn't reply, the banker moved haltingly for the door.

Tom Stamp was stunned by Clint's refusal of ten thousand dollars. Since banking—money—was his business, he naturally assumed that it would buy anything. Now his belief in that had been shaken, and he didn't know how to react.

Outside, he decided that when it was all over, Clint Adams would probably come to them and demand even more than ten thousand dollars. That's what he was doing. He was waiting until he had finished with the Bonds, and *then* he was going to demand his price.

Having reasoned it out, Tom Stamp felt a little better. He headed to the bank to go to work, with a stop first at Doc Moore's office to let him know what had happened.

"I don't believe that," Hailey said.

"Sure you do," Clint said. "He's a banker, Hailey. Money is everything to him, and he thinks that's the case with everyone. By now he's probably convinced himself that I'm going to ask for more later."

"No," she said, "you don't understand. I don't believe that he offered you ten thousand dollars."

"And you don't believe that I turned it down?" he added.

"Well . . . yes. It's more money than I've ever seen, Clint."

"At the risk of sounding like I'm preaching, Hailey,

my principles have never been for sale, for any price,"
he said. "Money doesn't mean that much to me. Oh,
I know I need it to eat, and to live, but as long as
I have enough for some supplies, and an occasional
hotel room, I'm satisfied. I've *never* hired my gun out
for money, and I don't intend to start now."

"I don't think I've ever met a man whose principles
meant as much to him as ten thousand dollars," she
said. "I'm impressed."

"Well, don't be," Clint said. "If I had that much
money, I wouldn't know what to do with it."

"Hey," she said, "I'd be more than willing to give
you some advice."

THIRTY-TWO

When they got back to the newspaper office they found Dr. Silas Moore waiting there for them.

"Come in, Silas," Hailey said, unlocking the door.

Inside Moore faced them and said, "I just left Tom Stamp. He's a very confused man."

"He told you," Clint said.

"Yes, he told me," Moore said. "I admire your principles, Mr. Adams. I don't claim to understand them, but I admire them."

"You all have the same problem," Clint said.

"What's that?"

"You think you're dealing with my reputation," Clint said. "What you're actually dealing with is me, and I'm just a man. I have beliefs, and I stick to them."

"I suppose you're right," Moore said, "and I suppose we've done you an injustice. If that's the case—if *I've* done you an injustice—I apologize."

"Never mind that," Clint said. "Did the council come to a decision?"

"Yes," Moore said. "We were just waiting for Tom to make his final offer. We accept *your* offer of help, in whatever form you see fit."

"All right," Clint said.

"What do we do now?" Moore said.

"I think I'll talk to each member of the council one at a time, Dr. Moore. I assume that you six men are the most influential men in town."

"I think that's safe to say."

"Then if I can convince you that you can deal with Marcus Bond yourselves, you should be able to convince others, as well."

"I suppose that would follow," Moore said, although he didn't seem too sure.

"Well, give me today to talk to each of you," Clint said. "After that, I'll know better what I'm dealing with."

"Very well," Moore said. "Do you want to talk to me now?"

"No," Clint said, "I think I'll save you for last, since you seem to be the spokesman for the group. Why don't we meet for a drink in the saloon tonight, around seven?"

"All right," Moore said. "I'll be there."

"Good."

Moore obviously expected Clint to say more, but when he didn't, the man moved toward the door awkwardly.

"I guess I'll be going. . . ."

"I'll see you this evening."

Moore nodded and went out the door.

"I've been meaning to ask you," Clint said, "is there anything between you and the doctor?"

"No."

"Was there ever anything?"

She hesitated a moment, then said, "No, not really.

I mean, I *think* he's in love with me, but I don't return his feelings."

"Okay," Clint said. "I just wanted to know."

"Who are you going to talk to first?" Hailey asked.

"The judge, I guess. Although Moore's the spokesman, the judge is probably the one the others listen to the most."

"I'd agree with that."

"Do you want to come along?"

"I hate being dependent . . ." she said. "Do you think Bond will come after me again?"

"No."

"But?"

"No buts," he said. "I just don't see it making any sense."

"Well, I don't want to have to follow you around all day."

"Do you have a gun?"

"No."

"All right. Go upstairs and in my saddlebags you'll find one. It's small, a Colt New Line, but it will stop a man cold. If need be, just keep pulling the trigger until the gun is empty."

"I hope it doesn't come to that," she said.

"Have you ever fired a gun?"

"I adhere to the adage that the pen is mightier than the gun," she said. "No, I have never fired a gun . . . at anything, let alone a man."

"Well, if Bond comes at you again, you'll fire it," he said.

"I hope it doesn't come to that," she said again.

"So do I," he said. "Will you get the gun and keep it on you?"

"Yes."

"All right, then," he said, putting his hand on her shoulder. "I'll see you later."

"Be careful," she said. "We don't know if Marcus Bond will come after you."

"I hope he doesn't," Clint said. "I'd have to kill him. That would free the town, but it really wouldn't help it. They'd be ripe for the next man or men who wanted to take it over. That's what I've got to get these men to see."

"Good luck."

"I guess I'll need it," he said and left.

THIRTY-THREE

Clint walked to the courthouse, which was the same building as the town hall. Judge Eric Bishop had an office right above the room where they had had the meeting of the town council. Since the judge was in his sixties, that was very convenient for him.

Clint entered the building, mounted the stairs, and walked up to the second floor. He went through the door that had writing on it that said, JUDGE ERIC BISHOP, ATTORNEY-AT-LAW. He found himself in a small reception room. There was a door opposite him that was open, and he could see the judge sitting behind his desk. He looked like he was dozing.

Clint walked to the door and knocked, jerking the judge awake.

"Who's that?" the old man said, squinting.

"It's Clint Adams, Judge. Is it all right if I come in?"

"Of course, Mr. Adams," the judge said. "Come in, come in. Have a seat."

Judge Eric Bishop must have once had a great, booming voice that would have served him well in court, both as a lawyer and as a judge. Now, however, it was a ghost of what it had once been.

Clint entered and sat opposite the judge.

"My clerk is out," the judge said.

Clint had noticed dust on the desk in the outer room, so it was his guess that the judge had not had a clerk for some time. The older man was either lying, or he actually thought he still had a clerk.

"What can I do for you, sir?"

"Well, I wanted to talk to you about Marcus Bond."

The judge leveled his watery eyes at Clint and said, "You don't have to convince me that you're right, young man. I would have ousted Bond myself long ago if I was only ten years younger. I agree that we have to get rid of this vermin on our own, but I've never been able to get the others to go along with it."

"Judge," Clint said, "all you need is for the other five members of the council to each pick up a rifle, and then get about ten or fifteen more men to do the same. Faced with twenty men, I think the Bonds would leave peaceably. They're only going to stay as long as the town is *willing* to remain beneath their thumb."

"That makes sense to me, son," the judge said. "Now talk to the others."

"I intend to, Judge," Clint said. "I just wanted to talk to you, first. I suspect the others respect what you have to say."

"Ha!" The judge laughed. "Once, maybe. Now they're all in love with the sound of their own voices. You heard Riley, and Stamp is just slightly better. The others—Cord and Carlisle—they're all right. They'll probably go along with you. I don't see Riley facing the Bonds, even with a hundred men behind him. And try and see if you can get that banker to come out from behind his desk with a gun. Ha!"

"And the doctor?"

"Ah, the good doctor," the judge said. "Probably the smartest man in town, but he just doesn't have any backbone. Won't even tell that Hailey Morgan woman that he's in love with her. 'Sides, he's a doctor. I don't know if you could get him to shoot a man. He's too used to healin' them up."

"So you think Carlisle and Cord will go along with me?" Clint asked.

"There's a good chance, yeah. Carlisle for sure, I think. You might have to convince Cord."

"But not the others?"

"Mr. Adams," the judge said, "this is all just my opinion, you understand. Yes, I can see that you do understand. You're going to talk to all of them anyway, aren't you?"

"That's right, Judge," Clint said, nodding. "That was my plan."

"Well then, get to it, son," Bishop said. "The quicker you start talkin', the quicker we can get rid of Marcus Bond and his sons."

"And then you'll need a new sheriff."

"A duly elected one," Bishop said, nodding. "That is, if I can find two men with backbone to run against each other."

Clint stood up and said, "Maybe by the time this is over, you'll know who those two men are."

"Couldn't convince you to take the job, could I?" Bishop asked. "I'd appoint you."

"No thanks, Judge," Clint said. "As soon as this is all wrapped up, I'll be heading out."

"Don't blame you," the judge said. "I'd leave myself, if I was only ten years younger."

Clint wondered how much time the judge spent behind his desk, dozing and wishing he was just ten years younger.

"I'll keep you informed, Judge."

"You do that, young man," the judge said, "you do that. And see if you can't get that pretty newspaper lady to come up and interview me, eh?" The old man had a twinkle in his eyes now. "Jesus, when I see her, it makes me wish I was ten years younger."

THIRTY-FOUR

Ben Bond sat in a wooden chair in front of the sheriff's office. His father was inside. He didn't know where his brothers were.

From his vantage point he saw all the comings and goings that morning. He saw Clint Adams and Hailey Morgan walk to the town hall. He saw Hailey Morgan walk to the café. Then he got up and stepped inside just before Kevin Riley walked by the office. He noticed him through the window.

"Riley just went by," Ben said to his father. "I thought he was coming in."

"He still might," Marcus said.

"I could go and ask him what was said at the meeting," Ben offered.

"No," Marcus said, "we'll wait, at least the rest of today. I think he'll come around on his own. Besides, I'm sure I *know* what the meeting was about."

"What?"

"They're tryin' to hire Adams to get rid of us."

Ben turned and looked at his father, a wolfish grin on his face.

"I hope he takes the job," he said.

"We'd be a lot better off if he didn't," Marcus said.

"Why?" Ben asked. "Pa, you ain't afraid of him, are you?"

"Not afraid, Ben," Marcus said slowly, "cautious. There's no reason to go up against this man unless we have to."

"I *want* to go up against him," Ben said.

"Ben," Marcus said, shaking his head, "he'd kill you."

"Pa—"

"I've seen you handle a gun, Ben," Marcus said. "You're good, but you're not anywhere near as good as this man is."

"We can find that out," Ben said.

"And we may have to," Marcus said, "but we're not gonna go after him. That's what he'll expect. We're gonna wait for him to come to us."

Ben started for the door.

"Where are you going?" Marcus asked.

"Just to sit out front," Ben said. "I want to keep an eye on the town."

"I'll tell you the same thing I told you yesterday, Ben," Marcus said. "Don't make a move against Adams unless I tell you."

"I hear you, Pa," Ben said.

He went outside and sat down in the chair again. He saw Tom Stamp walk by, and then come back again and stop at the doctor's office. After that he saw Doc Moore walk over to the newspaper office, and then saw Clint Adams and Hailey Morgan come back again and walk to the office.

He stood up and walked down the street until he was standing across from the newspaper office. Through

the window he saw Moore, Adams, and Hailey Morgan
talking. Were they firming up the deal? Had Adams
accepted whatever their offer was to sweep the Bonds
out of Allentown?

In spite of what his father had said, Ben Bond still
hoped that Adams *would* accept the offer. He wanted
to show his father, and the whole town, that he was a
better man than Clint Adams.

As the door to the newspaper office opened, Ben
moved into a doorway so he wouldn't be seen. Doc
Moore left, followed soon after by Clint Adams. That
left Hailey Morgan alone in the office.

Again he wondered, as he had the day before, if his
father had done anything else with the woman except
beat her up? Maybe he should go over himself and pay
her a visit?

He considered it seriously for several minutes, then
decided against it. His father might view it as a move
against Clint Adams, and Ben had been warned against
that. He decided to go back to the office and take his
seat out front. You could learn a lot just by watching,
and waiting.

THIRTY-FIVE

After leaving the judge's office, Clint went to talk to Sam Carlisle at the general store. As he entered, he saw Carlisle standing behind the counter. Seated, the man had not appeared very large, but standing, he was at least six four. He simply did not have the upper body of a man so tall. Seated, he appeared to be about five ten or so. Seeing him on his feet was a surprise.

Carlisle saw Clint looking at him and folded his arms across the chest.

"I know," he said. "I've heard every remark and comment I could possibly hear. I don't look this tall sitting down. Can we just get past that?"

"Sure," Clint said, "no problem."

"Thanks. What can I do for you?"

"I wanted to talk to you about Marcus Bond and his sons," Clint said.

"Are you ready to go up against them?" Carlisle asked. "I'll stand with you."

Carlisle, along with being so tall, was about forty-five or so. He appeared to be fit. It only remained to be seen if he could fire a gun.

"Not with *me*," Clint said, "but with your neighbor against the Bonds."

Carlisle stared at him for a few moments, then unfolded his arms and let them hang at his sides.

"That's not as appealing a prospect," he admitted.

"Mr. Carlisle—"

"Just Sam will do," Carlisle said.

"Sam . . . the other people in this town have to see that you and your fellow council members are willing to stand up for what's yours. If that happens, they'll follow along."

"How many of them?" Carlisle asked.

"You don't need the whole town," Clint said. "If we can find fifteen or twenty men to stand together, that would be enough. Marcus Bond and his sons would be foolish to stand against those kind of numbers."

Carlisle thought a moment and then said, "Yeah, suppose they would."

"I need your help, Sam," Clint said.

"You need *my* help?"

"Talk to some of the townspeople," Clint said. "Tell them that you and the council have decided it's time to get rid of the Bonds. Find out how many are willing to stand with you."

Carlisle rubbed his jaw and said, "Well, it'd just be talk for now."

"That's all," Clint said, and then added, "for now."

"What if Bond finds out what we're doin'?" Carlisle asked. "What if he comes after us, or me?"

"If that happens," Clint said, "if the Bonds move before we're ready, then I'll stand with you."

"Is that the truth?"

"I swear," Clint said. "What do you say?"

"Well, hell," Carlisle said, "I'll talk to some men I know who are as tired of having those four walk all over us like they own us as I am."

"Good," Clint said. "I'm going to talk to the others. With all of you working together, we might get this put together pretty quick."

"If you can get Tom Stamp and Kevin Riley to agree to this," the storekeeper said, "I'll be very surprised."

"You watch me, Sam," Clint said. "I'm going to talk to Stamp next."

"Good luck."

Clint left the general store and walked directly to the bank. He presented himself at one of the teller's cages and told the clerk that he wanted to speak to Mr. Stamp. Just minutes later, he was standing before Tom Stamp's desk.

"Mr. Adams," Stamp said, "have a seat." When Clint was seated the banker said, "Have you reconsidered my offer?"

"No, Mr. Stamp, I haven't," Clint said. He couldn't see himself ever calling the man Tom.

"Then why are you here?"

"To make you an offer," Clint said.

"I don't understand."

"I think you do," Clint said, "but I'll lay it out for you."

He spoke to Stamp just the way he had spoken to Carlisle, and even before he was finished, the man was shaking his head.

"I am not a man of violence, Mr. Adams," Stamp said when Clint finished talking. "I could no more step around this desk and pick up a gun than I could . . . well, sprout wings and fly."

"If a man came into this room," Clint said, "and pointed a gun at you, what would you do?"

Without missing a beat, Stamp said, "I suspect I would die rather abruptly."

"You don't have a gun in your desk, Mr. Stamp?"

"No."

Clint stared at the man.

"I find that hard to believe."

Stamp sat forward in his chair, looking excited.

"I think I'm understanding something, here," he said. "Just as I could not understand your refusal of ten thousand dollars, you can't understand my refusal to pick up a gun even to protect myself."

"That seems to be the case, yes," Clint said.

"Then I understand you better than I did earlier, Mr. Adams," Stamp said, with great satisfaction. "Yes indeed, I do. Do you understand my feelings?"

"Frankly," Clint said, "no."

"What puzzles you?"

"The concept of a man not defending himself," Clint said. "I've known men like that before, but they were usually men of the cloth."

"Mr. Adams," Stamp said. "Guns literally frighten me. If everyone in our society would stop carrying guns, I would be a much happier man. It has taken me many years to get to the point where I can walk the streets with people who are carrying guns. Indeed, that gun on your hip now is making me *very* nervous."

"What about Marcus Bond's guns?"

"They, too, make me nervous, but I am powerless to do anything about it."

"Maybe," Clint said slowly, "you are not as powerless as you think."

THIRTY-SIX

Clint took the time to explain very carefully to the bank manager what he had in mind. It was the same conversation he had with the judge, and with Sam Carlisle, but he was much more deliberate in delivering it to Tom Stamp.

"If I understand all of this correctly," Stamp said, "all I would have to do is *talk* to people?"

"That's it," Clint said.

"How will they feel about that?" Stamp asked. "I mean, a man who will not pick up a gun urging them to do so."

"I don't know," Clint said. "Why don't you find out?"

Stamp thought it over for a few moments, and then abruptly nodded his head.

From the bank Clint went to the feed and grain to talk to Will Cord. He gave the man the same pitch he had given the others, and Cord readily agreed.

"I've been waiting for someone to take the lead on this, Mr. Adams," Cord said. "I'm no leader, but I'm a helluva follower."

"I think you'll have to be a little of both this time,
Mr. Cord."

"Call me Will," Cord said, "and I'll give it my best
shot."

Clint shook hands with the man and told him he
would be in touch.

The last man to talk to was Kevin Riley. It was
everyone's opinion that he would never get Riley to
go along. It was Clint's opinion that since he had gotten virtually all of the others to agree, it didn't much
matter anymore whether Riley agreed or not. Still, he
was willing to give it a try.

As Clint entered the hardware store, Kevin Riley was
deep in conversation with a man, apparently a customer. Clint looked around for a few minutes while Riley
concluded his business. When the man headed for the
door, Clint walked up to the counter.

"Adams," Riley said.

"Mr. Riley."

"Come to recruit me for your plan?"

"What plan is that?"

Riley shrugged and said, "You know that better than
I do. You must have a plan."

"In fact, I do," Clint said.

"And you could use my help."

"That's exactly right."

"In fact," Riley said, "you want to put a gun in
my hand, point me at Marcus Bond and his sons, and
then fade into the background. Isn't that your plan,
Adams?"

"Not exactly," Clint said. "Are you willing to listen
or am I just going to be wasting my breath?"

For a moment he thought Riley was going to agree

that that's exactly what he'd be doing, but then the man shrugged, raised his hands, and said, "Okay, so I'll listen."

Quickly, Clint went over his proposed plan to collect enough guns to go against the Bonds.

"You're sayin' that we'll have so many guns that they won't even fight?" Riley summed up when he was done. "They'll just pull out?"

"That's what I'm hoping, yes."

"And tell me what happens if they *don't* pull out?" Riley said. "What happens if they're just crazy enough to put up a fight?"

Clint shrugged and said, "By sheer weight of numbers, they'll lose."

"And how many of us will lose also?" Riley asked. "How many of us will die? What's an acceptable percentage, Adams?"

"I don't know, Riley," Clint said, "but anyone who'll accept a gun will be given all of the possibilities. Anyone who wants to pull out can—including you."

"No," Riley said, "I won't pull out, because I'm not *in* to begin with. I'm not risking my life."

"You like things the way they are?" Clint asked.

"Hey," Riley said, "the way I see it, things could be a lot worse than they are now. So one of them comes in here every once in a while, picks out what he wants, and tells me to charge it. So they'll never pay for it, so what? That's better than bein' dead."

"Living under someone's thumb is not living, Riley," Clint said.

"You're wrong, Adams," Riley said, and he seemed vehement about it. "Being alive is living, that's all there is to it. And I intend to stay alive. You put together your little revolt, but don't count on me."

"That's okay," Clint said. "I wasn't counting on you in the first place. I just figured I'd give you a chance to go along."

"Well, thank you very much, but no thanks," Riley said. The door opened at that moment and a customer walked in. "Now if you don't mind, I have a business to run."

"Sorry to have taken up your time, Mr. Riley," Clint said and left.

THIRTY-SEVEN

Clint and Hailey had dinner at the same café, and he told her that all of the council members except Kevin Riley had agreed to take part in his plan.

"Even Tom Stamp?" she asked, surprised.

"Providing he doesn't have to handle a gun," Clint said.

"Well, that figures."

"It's good enough, Hailey," Clint said. "He'll talk to others. Actually, he's probably more help to us talking than he is trying to fire a gun."

"He's a good talker, all right," she said. "I have to tell you I'm surprised. I figured Carlisle and Cord would go along with you, but I had my doubts about the others." She folded her arms on the table, leaned forward, and said to him, "I guess you're a pretty convincing talker, too, aren't you?"

"I can be persuasive when I want to be," he said.

"Maybe you can persuade me to stay awake tonight when you get in bed with me?" She slid her foot up his leg under the table.

"I think that can be arranged," Clint said, "but first

135

I've got to meet with Silas Moore at the saloon."

"Just make sure one of those saloon girls doesn't change your mind," she said.

"No chance of that," he said. "I guarantee it."

Kevin Riley skulked down the street, hoping that no one would see him. He finally decided that instead of going to the sheriff's office and trying to enter through the front door without being seen, he'd sneak around the back and try to get in that way.

When he reached the back door, he found it locked and knocked on it. When no one responded, he closed his fist and pounded on it, flinching at the noise he was making. He was looking around to make sure no one was around when suddenly the door opened.

"Well, look who it is," Ben Bond said.

"Quick, let me in," Riley said nervously.

Ben stepped back and allowed Riley to enter, then closed the door and locked it.

"Is your father here?"

"Inside," Ben said. "He's been waiting for you."

"Waiting for me?" Riley asked, but Ben had already gone into the other room.

When Riley entered, Marcus Bond turned in his chair and sat back, regarding him silently. Ben was there, as was the strange one, George. Riley didn't see Red anywhere.

"What can I do for you, Riley?" Marcus asked. "That is, what do you think you can do for me?"

"It's Clint Adams, Marcus—" He stopped short when Marcus Bond's look turned hard and then said, "I mean, Sheriff."

"What about Adams?"

"He's got the other council members convinced that

they should talk to the men in town and convince *them* that it's time to get rid of you."

"Ha!" Marcus laughed. "The townspeople? I thought Adams was gonna come after us himself."

"He refused," Riley said. "Tom Stamp offered him a lot of money, but he turned it down. He said he doesn't hire out his gun."

"He's scared," Ben said, but Marcus raised his hand to silence his oldest son.

"So he's trying to rouse the townspeople, eh?" Marcus said. "He's not going to have much luck with that. If the men in this town wanted us gone, they would have tried to chase us a year ago."

"I don't know, Mar—uh, Sheriff," Riley said. "He's got the judge and Tom Stamp and Doc Moore talking to people. There's a chance they might listen."

"No chance," Marcus Bond said. "All right, Riley, you can go."

Riley stared at Marcus Bond, who had just dismissed him abruptly without so much as a thank you for the information.

"I wouldn't disregard this information, Sheriff," Riley said.

"I'll keep it in mind, Riley. That's all."

Ben moved up next to Riley and said, "Out."

Riley turned and started back the way he had entered.

"Go out the front," Marcus said.

"But—someone will see me."

Marcus just stared at him, and George stepped between him and the back door.

"The front," Ben Bond said, crowding Riley so that he had no choice but to move toward the front door.

"Ben, someone will see me," he said under his breath.

"Riley," Ben said, "that's your problem. Out."

Ben opened the door and shoved Riley outside, slamming it behind him.

He turned to his father and said, "Well? Can I go after Adams now?"

Marcus looked at Ben, then at George, and said, "Yeah, Ben, I think it's time to show the town that even someone like the Gunsmith can't stand against us. It will get rid of *any* ideas they might have about banding together."

"Finally!" Ben said, putting his hand on the doorknob.

"Ben!"

"What?"

Marcus stared at his oldest son and said, "We're gonna do it my way."

"Pa—"

"Ben," Marcus said, shaking his head. In almost a whisper he said again, "My way."

THIRTY-EIGHT

Clint was sitting in the saloon, nursing a beer that Rayanne had brought him, when Dr. Silas Moore walked in. He looked around, spotted Clint, and started toward him, weaving his way between tables and people. Along the way he stopped by Rayanne, speaking to her briefly, and then he continued until he reached Clint's table.

"Sorry I'm late," he said. "I had a patient."

"No problem."

Moore sat down, and Rayanne appeared with a glass and a bottle of whiskey. Moore took the time to pour himself a drink, down it, then pour a second and set it down next to the bottle.

"Why do you do that?" Clint asked.

"What?"

"Drink the first one and then leave the second one on the table next to the bottle?"

"I'm trying to stop," Moore said.

Rayanne looked at Clint and asked, "Do you want a fresh beer?"

"Sure, Rayanne," Clint said, pushing the lukewarm remnants of his first one away, "why not?"

"Be right back." She grabbed up the old glass and went to get a new one.

"So, what happened?" Moore asked. "Did any of them go for it? Besides Carlisle, I mean."

"All of them."

"All of them?" Moore asked, in surprise.

"All but Riley."

"Ah," Moore said. "I knew Riley wouldn't agree, but Tom Stamp?"

Clint explained to Moore the provision under which Stamp was helping them.

"Well, that makes sense," Moore said. "Actually, I might even make you the same deal myself. As a doctor, I don't feel I can justify picking up a gun and shooting someone."

"That'll be up to you, Doctor," Clint said.

Rayanne returned with the fresh beer, set it down next to Clint, gave him a hip bump, and then sashayed away.

"The girl likes you," Moore said.

"She's very attractive," Clint said.

The two men matched stares, and Clint wondered if Hailey's name was going to come up between them.

Ultimately, it did not.

"What's going to happen if word gets to Marcus Bond?" Moore asked.

"Do you think it will?" Clint asked.

"It's possible."

"Who'll tell him, Doc?" Clint asked.

Moore didn't answer.

"Riley?"

Moore made a pained face and said, "I wouldn't be surprised. I would hope not, but . . ." he finished lamely, shaking his head.

"If Riley goes to Bond," Clint said, "he'll come after me—or send one of his sons after me."

"To show the rest of us that even you can't stand against him," Moore said.

"Right."

"And if that happens?"

"I guess we'll just have to wait and see," Clint said, "won't we?"

"I guess so," Dr. Moore said. "Well, I'd better be going."

"Have you spoken to anyone today, Doc?"

"A few men," Moore said. "I have to tell you, there's considerable resistance."

"Well . . . keep working on them," Clint said. "Someone in this town has to have some guts, don't you think?"

"You'd think so, wouldn't you?" Moore said.

Moore weaved his way to the door and left. Rayanne immediately came over to the table. Clint looked up at her, and she was smiling. She had a lovely face, a long, smooth neck, and the slopes of her breasts were like cream.

"How's the beer?" she asked.

"It's fine."

"Can I get you . . . anything else?"

He smiled at her and said, "Under other circumstances, Rayanne, you could do a *lot* for me, but not tonight, I'm afraid."

She looked disappointed, thrusting her lush lower lip out provocatively.

"Maybe another night?" she asked.

"Maybe," he said. "We'll see."

"Oh well," Rayanne said, "give me a holler if you need anything."

She walked away swaying her hips. He watched briefly, then turned his attention inward.

The more he thought about it, the more he felt that someone was going to get word to Marcus Bond. It might be Riley, or it might be someone else. Maybe someone who figured if Bond went after Clint, then Clint would kill him and the whole problem would be solved.

Well, Clint felt sure that Marcus Bond wouldn't come after him himself. He'd send one of his sons . . . but which one?

THIRTY-NINE

When Clint returned to the office of *The Allentown Gazette*, he expected to find Hailey upstairs, perhaps resting. Instead, she was seated at her desk, and the press was running. Clint had to come up behind her and tap her on the shoulder. She whirled about quickly, eyes wide, pointing the Colt New Line at him. He reached out and quickly snatched the gun from her hand, then put his hand on her shoulder to calm her down.

She took a moment to regain her breath, then stood up and walked to the press, shutting it off.

"I'm sorry," he said.

"No, I'm sorry," she said. "I could have shot you."

"It's all right," he said, putting the gun down on her desk. "Why aren't you upstairs resting?"

Suddenly, her fear was gone, replaced by excitement.

"I'll show you," she said.

She reached into the press and came out with a page. She held it up proudly for him to read. He had only to read the headline.

ALLENTOWN CLEANS HOUSE, it said, and he could just imagine what it was about.

"Is that dated?" he asked.

"No," she admitted, "not yet."

"I see," he said. "You're hoping that it will happen—when? Within the next week or so?"

"The next few days," she said. "Don't you think so?"

"I wouldn't count on it," he said.

"Why not?"

"We've got to wait for everyone's initial resistance to fade," Clint said. "No matter who the council talks to, Hailey, those people are going to have to think before they make their decision."

"Oh, it doesn't matter," she said. "A few days, a week, I'll have my story ready—and what a story!"

"Does your story make mention of me?"

She lowered the page and set it down, then looked at him.

"That's something I was going to ask you about, Clint," she said. "Can I mention you in the story?"

"You think having me in there will make for a good story?"

"It will make for a great story," she said.

"No," he said, "I think you're wrong. I think *not* having me in it will make it a great story."

She frowned.

"What do you mean?"

"I mean a town being led in some sort of a revolt by a man with a reputation is a story," he said. "But a town rising up on its own, with no stranger to lead them, that makes a great story. Think about it."

"I am thinking about it," she said. He could see that she was. Although she was looking in his direction, she wasn't seeing him. Rather, she was seeing her story as it might be.

Suddenly, her eyes focused, and she looked at him.

"Are you sure you were never a newspaperman?" she asked him.

"Never."

"You're a natural," she said. "That *is* a great story. You don't have to worry. I won't mention you."

"I wasn't worried," he said. Concerned, he added to himself, but not worried.

She reached for the press to turn it back on, but he stepped forward and caught her hand.

"Time to rest," he said.

"But—"

"This story doesn't have to be ready by tomorrow, right?" he said.

"Well—"

"That means you have time to go upstairs and rest," he insisted.

She stared at him, then smiled and said, "Only if you'll come up and rest with me."

"If I come up," he said, "we're not going to rest."

"I know. . . ."

FORTY

Upstairs Hailey allowed Clint to undress her this time, and he did it slowly.

"Why didn't you let me do this before?" he asked.

"I wasn't bruised and battered before," she said. "I—I like to undress myself."

"I'll make this as painless as possible," he promised.

He removed her shirt then and leaned forward to gently lick and kiss her breasts, mindful of the bruises on them. She moaned as he took her nipples into his mouth and rolled them with his tongue.

Gently, he ran his hand over her bruised side and unbuttoned her pants. He slid them down her thighs and tossed them away when she stepped out of them. He ran his hands over her thighs, leaned forward, and kissed them gently.

He removed her undergarments, and then she was totally naked. She sat on the bed and then lay down on her back. He undressed and joined her on the bed.

"Just lie still," he told her. "Let me do all the work."

She nodded and closed her eyes.

Clint used his mouth, his tongue, his hands on her, touching her, teasing her until she begged him to enter her. Instead, he moved down so that his face was between her legs and began to work on her with his tongue. She gasped when he placed a kiss between her legs, then began to lick her and suck her. Finally, he slid his hands beneath her, cupped her buttocks, lifted her off the bed, and took her clit in his mouth. It was just moments later that she was moaning and gasping and slamming her closed fists down on the mattress.

He lowered her to the bed, raised himself over her, and entered her, slowly, so slowly that it was almost painful for both of them.

"Oh, God, Clint . . ." she said. She tried to lift her legs to wrap them around him, but the movement caused pain to lance through her side. She gasped in pain, lowered her legs, and then gasped again as he slid into her all the way.

"Easy . . ." he told her, "easy. . . ."

He held his own weight on his arms and legs so that he wouldn't hurt her and slid in and out of her that way. She moaned and cried, from both the pleasure and the frustration of not being able to just clutch him to her. She raised her hands over her head as he bent to kiss her breasts, and then she got some sort of satisfaction from grasping his head and clutching it to her. She moved her hips against him, even though it hurt slightly, and then the pleasure was just rushing through her so that the pain no longer existed . . . and he exploded inside of her. . . .

FORTY-ONE

Clint woke abruptly and knew that someone was in the building. The room was dark, and he waited, urging his night vision to clear. Finally, when he thought he could see well enough, he sat up and eased himself from the bed. He didn't want to wake Hailey, because she might wake noisily, warning whoever was lurking about.

His gun belt was hanging on the bedpost, and he slid his gun from the holster. He took a quick look at the window in the room, and it was secure. Whoever was moving around had not yet reached the second floor, so he was fairly certain the person hadn't gotten in through the rear window. That meant that the intruder had probably forced the door downstairs and entered that way. There was only one way to get to the second floor, and that was the stairway.

Clint moved into the other room, to the head of the steps, and waited.

Marcus Bond sat behind his desk in his office, wondering silently if he had done the right thing, if he had sent the right son after Clint Adams.

He was alone in his office so he got up and paced, which he might not have done in front of his other two boys. He could have sent all three boys after Adams, but he wanted it done quietly. The three of them would never have been able to break into the newspaper office quietly. One man, though, could.

Bond was waiting for the outcome. As long as he didn't hear a shot within the next fifteen or twenty minutes, everything would be fine. If he *did* hear a shot, then everything would come to a head tomorrow.

He stopped pacing, walked back to his desk, and sat down to wait.

Clint realized that he was naked, but he hadn't wanted to take the time to pull his pants on. He was hunkered down at the head of the stairs, looking down and waiting for someone to come into view. He wasn't yet sure what he would do when that person did. Should he simply fire, or give the person a chance to give up?

He felt fairly certain that the intruder would turn out to be one of Marcus Bond's sons. It would be interesting to find out which one it was. Clint's money was on the oldest, Ben.

He heard the floorboards downstairs creaking. It was pitch-dark, so there were no shadows to be cast. Still, his instinct told him that the intruder was approaching the steps. He moved off to the side, so that he wasn't in plain sight. Also, he didn't want to get hit by a lucky shot, so he pressed his back to the wall and held his gun at the ready. He offered up a silent prayer that Hailey wouldn't wake up at the wrong time and call out to him.

There was someone at the foot of the steps. The

person mounted the first step, then the second, and then the third, slowly. Clint waited patiently until the intruder was at the halfway point. From there, there was no place to go.

"Stand fast," he said, pointing the gun.

The man on the steps stopped.

"If you're carrying a gun, let me hear it fall down the stairs," Clint instructed.

There was no movement.

"Do it!"

There was a moment of silence, and then he heard something tumble down the stairs. He hoped it was a gun. Whatever it was, though, it woke Hailey.

"Clint?"

"Light a lamp, Hailey," Clint called out, "and bring it here."

"What's going on?"

"Just do it, honey."

He heard a match strike behind him, and then light filled the room. It came over his shoulder, and he cast a shadow against the wall. He still couldn't see the person on the steps, but whoever it was wasn't talking and wasn't moving.

"Clint?" He heard Hailey behind him, closer now, and the light was growing brighter.

"Hailey, just hold the lamp—" he started, but suddenly the figure on the steps moved. He threw something, and Clint flinched and fired just as a knife pierced his left shoulder.

"Shit," he said as the figure on the steps tumbled down the stairs backward.

"Clint?"

Hailey ran to him and gasped when she saw the knife sticking out of his shoulder.

Clint sat down on the floor and lowered the gun. He took a breath, tried to rise, but couldn't. His legs felt weak.

"All right," he said to her, "go down the steps and see if he's dead."

"But you're hurt—"

"Hailey, come on," he said. "Do as I say."

She eased past him and walked down the stairs with the lamp. She was as naked as Clint was. She stopped at the body, hesitated, then reached for the man and turned him over.

"He's dead," she called to him, looking up the stairs.

"Do you know who he is?"

"Yes," she said. "It's George Bond."

"George," he said, nodding. "Okay, Hailey, you've got to get dressed and go get Doc Moore for me. Do it fast, 'cause I think I'm going to . . . uh . . . pass . . . out. . . ."

FORTY-TWO

"I just hope he didn't use the same knife he used to gut all his small animals," Silas Moore said. "You could be looking at some serious infection if he did."

"Great," Clint said.

"Okay," Moore said, finishing the dressing.

Clint was sitting in a chair at Hailey's place. The body of George Bond had been removed by some men Moore had arranged for, men who had already agreed to help.

"You should get into bed and stay there for a few days," Moore said.

"Maybe later today," Clint said, "after we've taken care of the Bonds."

"That's going to happen today?" Hailey asked.

She was standing off to one side, fully dressed. She and Moore had helped Clint pull on a pair of jeans.

The first thing Moore had done upon arrival with Hailey had been to remove the knife and stop the bleeding. The second thing Clint had him do was arrange to move the body.

"I have to bandage you," Moore had said.

"After you take care of the body," Clint said. "Bond probably heard the shot, but if we can keep him in the dark about exactly what happened, it will work to our advantage. Not hearing will make him nervous."

Moore agreed. He went and got three men who carried the body out the back door and took it to the undertaker's office. While they did that, Moore bandaged Clint's wound.

They heard someone coming up the stairs, and Willy Rose came into view. He was one of the men who had carried the body away.

"The body is at the undertaker's," he told them.

"All right, Willy, thanks," Moore said.

"We need to get everyone together at first light," Clint said to Willy and Moore. "Do we know how many men we have?"

"Not until we put them all together in the same place and take a count," Moore said.

"Okay, we'll do that in the morning. Talk to Carlisle. He has some guns in his store, and we can give them out to anyone who doesn't have his own."

"Are we gonna face the sheriff and his boys *tomorrow*?" Willy asked.

"Yes, you are," Clint said. "It's as good a time as any."

Willy swallowed nervously, nodded, and said, "Well, I'll be ready."

"Good, Willy," Moore said. "I knew we could count on you. Pass the word that we'll meet at the town hall. The meeting room might be big enough to hold us all."

"Yes, sir," Willy said.

"We'll see you then."

Willy nodded and went back down the stairs.

Moore turned to Clint and said, "What if we don't have enough men?"

"Ten should be enough," Clint said. "Bond is down to himself and two sons. If you've got ten, that should be plenty."

"I hope so," Moore said. He looked at Hailey and said, "He should rest, at least until morning."

"He will," she said.

Moore nodded, said, "I'll see you both in the morning," and left.

"Come on," Hailey said to Clint. "Into bed."

She helped him to the bed and sat next to him.

"Who was George after, Clint, you or me?"

"Me, I'd say," Clint said. "Why come after you?"

"But . . . how did he know you were here?"

"I don't know," Clint said. "I figured Kevin Riley must have told him what we were planning, but Riley didn't know I was here."

"Who did?" she asked.

He looked at her, then said, "That's something we'll have to figure out later. Hailey, I want to say that I'm sorry."

"About what?"

"About letting George Bond get in here," he said. "I was lax. I mean, if he had managed to get upstairs before I heard him—"

"But he didn't," she said, "and it isn't your fault that he got as far as he did, it's mine."

"Yours?" he asked. "How do you figure that?"

She put her hand on his chest and said, "I tired you out so much that you slept soundly."

She leaned over and kissed him, and when he reached for her with his right hand she said, "Oh no, you need rest. Doctor's orders."

"All right, nurse," he said.

She doused the lamp and lay down next to him.

"Do you think they'll try again tonight?" she asked in the dark.

"No," he said. "Marcus Bond doesn't know for sure what happened tonight. He'll wait until morning to find out."

"Well," she said, "just in case, I've got that little gun you gave me right here."

"That's good," Clint said. His gun, too, was on the floor rather than the bedpost, where it would be easier for him to get to. He didn't tell her, but even though he was lying down, he intended to stay awake the rest of the night.

Hailey Morgan had the same intention.

FORTY-THREE

Marcus Bond heard the shot, but he didn't move from his office. He waited . . . and waited . . . and waited, and when George didn't return, he *knew* what had happened.

He had sent George because he thought he'd be able to kill Adams with his knife. That way the town wouldn't be alerted, and in the morning Adams would just turn up dead. The Gunsmith dying that way would have scared the hell out of everyone.

The door to the office opened, and Ben and Red walked in.

"We heard the shot," Ben said.

"Is George dead?" Red asked.

"I don't know," Marcus said.

"Shouldn't we find out?" Ben asked.

"We will find out," Marcus said, "in the morning."

"Pa—" Red started.

"They may have just caught him," Marcus said. "If they did, he won't talk to them. In the morning I'll find out what happened. After all, I am the sheriff."

"Right," Ben said, frowning.

"Now get out," Marcus said. "I'll see you in the morning."

They both left the office.

"What should we do, Ben?" Red asked outside.

"You do as you're told, Red," Ben said. "Go back to the house."

"Where are you going?"

"To Meg's."

"But Ben—"

"Go on home, Red," Ben said.

As Ben walked away, Red thought to himself that he didn't know where "home" was.

When Red returned to the house, Nancy was waiting for him.

"What happened, Red?" she asked.

"I think George is dead, Nancy."

He walked to the sofa and sat down heavily.

"Where's Pa?" she asked.

"In his office."

"And Ben?"

"He went to Meg's."

She sat down next to him and put her hand on his arm. She was almost vibrating with the urgency and excitement she was feeling.

"It's time, Red."

"Time for what?" he asked, distracted.

She grabbed his face in one hand, cupping his chin, and turned it to face her.

"Time to leave, Red," she said. "If George is dead, that means they know—this Clint Adams you told me about, he *knows* that Pa sent George after him. He's gonna come after Pa."

"Me and Ben," Red said, "we have to help Pa."

"We have to leave, Red," she said. "It could be our only chance. Even if Pa wins, he'll be too busy to worry about us leavin'."

"But, if Pa gets killed—"

"Then he can't come after us, at all," she said. "Don't you see? It's now or never."

Red turned away, a worried look on his face. He started chewing his bottom lip.

"Come on, Red," she said. "You know I'm right. Let's go . . . now!"

The first thing Ben Bond did when he entered Meg Black's house was to backhand her across the face, knocking her to the floor.

"What was that for?" she asked from the floor. The words were out before she could stop herself.

"Never mind what it was for," he said. "Just get undressed."

"Ben—"

"You want to get hit again?" he asked.

"N-no. . . ."

"Then get undressed, damn it."

She started to undress, but she wasn't fast enough for him. He grabbed her and tore the dress she was wearing from her, leaving her naked except for a few strips of cloth. In tearing the dress he scratched her, three livid red marks across one breast. They stung.

Meg thought about the gun in her drawer as Ben grabbed her and threw her on the bed. . . .

It was early the next morning when little Kyle Martin, eight years old, heard the first shot, and then the second shot, coming from Meg Black's house. Kyle, being the curious little boy that he was, went up to the house and peered in all the windows, until he found the bedroom window. When he saw what was inside, he ran for Doc Moore.

FORTY-FOUR

The next morning Hailey helped Clint put on his shirt. He winced as he moved his arm.

"Hurt?" she asked.

"Sore," he said. "Now I know how you felt."

"It's hardly the same thing," she said. "You were stabbed, for God's sake."

"Sore is sore," he said.

"I still think you should stay here."

"Come on," he said. "We can finish this all today, if we're lucky."

"Sure," she said, "you could be gone by tomorrow morning, right? Let's get going, by all means."

She went down the stairs ahead of him before he could say a word.

When they reached the town hall there were already half a dozen men in the meeting room. Unfortunately, four of them were Carlisle, Cord, Stamp, and the judge. Only two of them were carrying guns. The other two men were Willy Rose and one of the men who had helped move George Bond's body.

As they entered, the judge said, "Willy Rose told us

what happened during the night, Mr. Adams."

"One less Bond to worry about," Carlisle said.

Clint turned as the door opened and two more men
with guns walked in.

"Where is Doc Moore?" he asked the judge.

"I haven't seen him this morning," the judge said.

"Sam?"

"Nope," Carlisle said. None of the other men had
seen him either.

Three more men arrived and shook hands with
Stamp. Obviously the banker had come through. There
were now a dozen men in the room, almost all of them
carrying guns.

"We're lookin' good," Carlisle said, "but where's
Doc?"

As if on cue, the door opened and Doc Moore came in.
He seemed surprised at the number of men who were in
the room.

"Glad to see you all here," he said.

" 'Bout time we did somethin' for ourselves," one of
the men said, and the others echoed the sentiment.

"This looks like it's going to work," the doctor said.

"Where have you been?" Clint asked.

"Step outside with me for a minute, will you?" Moore
said to Clint.

As they stepped outside, they passed two more men
coming in with guns. Both shook Doc Moore's hand.

"What's going on?" Clint asked.

"Ben Bond is dead."

"What?"

"So is Meg Black."

"What the hell happened?"

"It looks like Meg shot him while he was asleep, and
then turned the gun on herself," Moore said. "There

were scratches and bruises on her body." He shrugged helplessly and said, "I guess she just had enough."

"Does Marcus know?" Clint asked.

"I don't know."

"That means it's down to Marcus and Red," Clint said. "Just the two of them."

"How many men have we got?" Moore asked.

"With the two who just went in," Clint said, "and you, fifteen."

"Sounds like enough to me," Moore said.

"Me, too," Clint said. "Let's do it."

Marcus Bond spent the night in his office, and when he woke up he was surprised not to find Ben and Red there.

He made a pot of coffee, but when they still didn't show up he went looking for them.

When he got to the house, he entered, calling out, "Red! Hey, Red!" When Red didn't answer, he shouted, "Nancy!"

When Nancy didn't answer, he went to her room. She wasn't there, and her drawers were empty. Obviously, she had left, but the question was, did she take Red with her?

Marcus ran to the livery stable and found both Nancy and Red's horses gone. George's was still there, though, and so was Ben's.

He left the livery and ran to Meg Black's house. When no one answered the door, he kicked it open.

"Ben!" he shouted. "Where the hell are you?"

By this time the bodies of Ben Bond and Meg Black had already been removed, so when Marcus Bond entered the bedroom, all he saw were bed sheets covered with blood.

"Jesus!" he said.

One of them had gone crazy, either Ben or the bitch.

He left the house and ran back to his office. He was approaching it when he saw the group of men coming from the other direction.

Clint and Hailey moved across the street, so they could watch. Judge Bishop and Tom Stamp were on the other side. Doc Moore had decided to lead the armed men to the sheriff's office. Having eleven men behind you helped you find backbone, Clint thought, but still, he had to give the man some credit.

Clint enjoyed being the observer for once, even though the wound in his shoulder was a painful reminder that, in the long run, he had been much more than that.

He saw Marcus Bond trotting down the street, and then saw him stop short when he saw Moore and the other men.

"Watch—" Clint started, but Hailey shushed him.

She was taking notes.

FORTY-FIVE

"What's goin' on?" Marcus Bond shouted. "You people go back to your homes!"

"You can't bully us anymore, Marcus," Moore called out.

"What are you talkin' about?" Marcus said. "What do you want?"

"We want you to leave town," Sam Carlisle said. "Now, Marcus."

"You're crazy," Bond said. "I'm the sheriff. Wait until my boys—"

"Your boys aren't coming," Moore said. "George is dead. He was killed by Clint Adams last night, after you sent him out to kill Adams."

"Ben," Marcus said, looking around, "Ben will be here."

"Ben's dead, too, Marcus," Moore said, "killed by a woman he abused once too often."

"Meg Black?" Bond asked.

Moore nodded.

"She killed him, and then herself."

"Where's Red?" Marcus said. "What did you do with Red?"

Moore looked around, then said, "We haven't seen Red, Marcus. Is he gone?"

Marcus Bond raised his hands helplessly and then let them drop to his sides. He looked very old at that point.

"Red's gone," Marcus said. "He left with Nancy."

"Your daughter's gone, too, Marcus?" Moore said. "Then you're all alone, aren't you?"

Marcus Bond started looking around him frantically, but there was no one there to help him.

"Leave town, Marcus," Will Cord said. "Maybe you can find Red and Nancy."

Marcus looked at the dozen armed men again and then pointed.

"No," he said, "I'm not leavin'. I'll tell everyone what you did."

It wasn't clear whom he was talking to.

"Keep your hands away from your guns, Marcus," Carlisle said.

"Throw your badge down," Cord said.

"It's all over, Marcus," Moore said.

"No," Marcus said.

At the time, Clint wasn't sure whether the man had made a move for his gun or not, but someone in the group fired a shot, and then the others started firing.

Marcus Bond jerked about in the center of the street like a puppet on a string as the bullets struck his body. He didn't even step back, just jerked in place until they stopped firing, and then his riddled corpse fell to the ground.

"And that's *thirty*," Hailey Morgan said, using the journalist's word for *the end*.

FORTY-SIX

Clint stayed a week while his shoulder healed. Hailey wrote her story, and Allentown started looking for a new sheriff. The story from *The Allentown Gazette* was picked up by some other newspapers, and a telegram from the East informed Hailey that it had even made it that far.

Clint moved to the hotel to heal up, but Hailey came to stay with him at night.

The day before he was to leave, he had lunch with Hailey at the café.

"Do you have to leave tomorrow?" she asked.

"I'm overdue to leave, Hailey," he said. "You know that."

"Yes, I do," she said, "and I won't ask you to stay. In fact, I'm fighting to keep from asking you to sit still for an interview."

"Good," he said, "keep fighting."

"You know," she said, "there's something about all of this that still bothers me."

"What?"

"I still don't know how Marcus knew to send George after you at my place."

165

Clint shrugged.

"Maybe we'll never know that."

"And who was Marcus talking to when he said he was going to 'tell everyone what *you* did'?"

"Something else we'll probably never know."

After breakfast Hailey went to her office to work on her next edition. Clint promised to meet her for dinner.

What he had said to her wasn't quite the truth. Clint thought he knew the answers to both questions. At one point he thought he could leave town without verifying it, but now he knew he couldn't. He had to wrap it all up before he left.

He went to talk to Sam Carlisle first, and then to Kevin Riley.

After he found out what he needed to know from Carlisle and Riley, Clint went to talk to Doc Moore.

"Clint," Moore said as Clint entered the office, "how's the shoulder?"

"Fine."

"Are you leaving tomorrow?"

"Yes."

"Want me to take a look before you go? I have time."

"Why not?"

They went into the examination room, and Clint removed his shirt.

"Any luck with finding a new sheriff?" he asked.

"I don't know, for sure," Moore said, examining the wound. "That's the judge's department."

"You know, I talked to Sam Carlisle today."

"Oh? About what?"

"About who fired the first shot at Marcus," he said. "I've been wondering about it, and I finally had to ask."

"Oh?"

"You did, Doc," Clint said. "I didn't even know you had a gun on you that day."

Moore looked at Clint's face, then stepped back and said, "It's healing nicely. You can get dressed."

"Doc?"

Moore turned and walked away. He washed his hands and turned to face Clint while he was drying them.

"I decided to carry a gun like everyone else," he said finally. "It was only fair."

"Why did you fire?"

"He went for his gun."

Clint buttoned his shirt and said, "That's what I thought, too, but as I think back on it, I don't think he did. He was sort of helpless at that point. I don't think he even knew what he was doing with his hands."

"Well . . . it wasn't my kind of situation. Maybe I misread it."

"I don't think you did."

"What do you mean?"

"Come on, Doc," Clint said. "You shot him on purpose."

"Why would I do that?"

"Because he said he was going to give you away," Clint said, "tell what you had done."

Moore laughed.

"He wasn't talking to me when he said that."

"I think he was."

"What could he possibly have given away?"

"The fact that it was you who told him that I was staying with Hailey," Clint said. "That's how he knew to send George after me there and not at the hotel."

"That wasn't me, Clint," Moore said. "That was Kevin Riley."

"No," Clint said, "I spoke to Kevin Riley today. He admits that he told Bond we were banding together to come after him, but he denies telling Bond that I was staying with Hailey." Clint tucked in his shirt, pointed at the doctor, and said, "That was you, Doc."

"And you believe him?"

"That's right," Clint said. "I believe him."

Moore tossed away the towel he had been using to dry his hands and said, "Why would I do that, Clint?"

"Jealousy," Clint said. "A common enough motive for anything."

Moore remained silent, neither confirming nor denying.

"Doc?"

"Are you going to tell Hailey?" Moore finally said, admitting his guilt.

"No," Clint said, walking to the door.

"Why not?"

"I think Hailey is smart enough to make her own decisions about men," Clint said. "Even without knowing this, she'll make the right decision about you, Doc. Count on it."

"Clint—"

"Good-bye, Doc," Clint said. "I'm leaving in the morning. I, uh, don't want to see you again between now and then. Understood?"

Moore nodded and said, "I understand."

"Good," Clint said and walked out.

Now he knew it all. Why didn't he feel satisfied? Because knowing the truth wasn't always satisfying, that's why. Because he had been hoping that he was wrong.

"Damn."

Watch for

DEADLY GOLD

138th novel in the exciting GUNSMITH series
from Jove

Coming in June!

Omaha, Nebraska, Early Spring, 1866

Construction Engineer Glenn Gilchrist stood on the melting surface of the frozen Missouri River with his heart hammering his rib cage. Poised before him on the eastern bank of the river was the last Union Pacific supply train asked to make this dangerous river crossing before the ice broke to flood south. The temperatures had soared as an early chinook had swept across the northern plains and now the river's ice was sweating like a fat man in July. A lake of melted ice was growing deeper by the hour and there was still this last critical supply train to bring across.

"This is madness!" Glenn whispered even as the waiting locomotive puffed and banged with impatience while huge crowds from Omaha and Council Bluffs stomped their slushy shorelines to keep their feet warm. Fresh out of the Harvard School of Engineering, Glenn had measured and remeasured the depth and stress-carrying load of the rapidly melting river yet still could not be certain if it would

support the tremendous weight of this last supply
train. But Union Pacific's vice president, Thomas
Durant, had given the bold order that it was to
cross, and there were enough fools to be found willing to man the train and its supply cars, so here
Glenn was, standing in the middle of the Missouri
and about half sure he was about to enter a watery
grave.

Suddenly, the locomotive engineer blasted his steam
whistle and leaned out his window. "We got a full head
of steam and the temperature is risin', Mr. Gilchrist!"

Glenn did not hear the man because he was imag-
ining what would happen the moment the ice broke
through. Good Lord, they could all plunge to the bottom of Big Muddy and be swept along under the ice for
hundreds of miles to a frozen death. A vision flashed
before Glenn's eyes of an immense ragged hole in the
ice fed by two sets of rails feeding into the cold dark-
ness of the Missouri River.

The steam whistle blasted again. Glenn took a deep
breath, raised his hand, and then chopped it down
as if he were swinging an ax. Cheers erupted from
both riverbanks and the locomotive jerked tons of rails,
wooden ties, and track-laying hardware into motion.

Glenn swore he could feel the weakening ice heave
and buckle the exact instant the Manchester locomotive's thirty tons crunched its terrible weight onto the
river's surface. Glenn drew in a sharp breath. His eyes
squinted into the blinding glare of ice and water as the
railroad tracks swam toward the advancing locomotive
through melting water. The sun bathed the rippling
surface of the Missouri River in a shimmering bril-
liance. The engineer began to blast his steam whistle
and the crowds roared at each other across the frozen

expanse. Glenn finally expelled a deep breath, then started to backpedal as he motioned the locomotive forward into railroading history.

Engineer Bill Donovan was grinning like a fool and kept yanking on the whistle cord, egging on the cheering crowds.

"Slow down!" Glenn shouted at the engineer, barely able to hear his own voice as the steam whistle continued its infernal shriek.

But Donovan wasn't about to slow down. His unholy grin was as hard as the screeching iron horse he rode and Glenn could hear Donovan shouting to his firemen to shovel faster. Donovan was pushing him, driving the locomotive ahead as if he were intent on forcing Glenn aside and charging across the river to the other side.

"Slow down!" Glenn shouted, backpedaling furiously.

But Donovan wouldn't pull back on his throttle, which left Glenn with just two poor choices. He could either leap aside and let the supply train rush past, or he could try to swing on board and wrestle its control from Donovan. It might be the only thing that would keep the ice from swallowing them alive.

Glenn chose the latter. He stepped from between the shivering rails, and when Donovan and his damned locomotive charged past drenching him in a bone-chilling sheet of ice water, Glenn lunged for the platform railing between the cab and the coal tender. The locomotive's momentum catapulted him upward to sprawl between the locomotive and tender.

"Dammit!" he shouted, clambering to his feet. "The ice isn't thick enough to take both the weight and a pounding! You were supposed to . . ."

Glenn's words died in his throat an instant later when the ice cracked like rifle fire and thin, ragged schisms fanned out from both sides of the tracks. At the same time, the rails and the ties they rested upon rolled as if supported by the storm-tossed North Atlantic.

"Jesus Christ!" Donovan shouted, his face draining of color and leaving him ashen. "We're going under!"

"Throttle down!" Glenn yelled as he jumped for the brake.

The locomotive's sudden deceleration threw them both hard against the firebox, searing flesh. The fireman's shovel clattered on the deck as his face corroded with terror and the ice splintered outward from them with dark tentacles.

"Steady!" Glenn ordered, grabbing the young man's arm because he was sure the kid was about to jump from the coal tender. "Steady now!"

The next few minutes were an eternity but the ice held as they crossed the center of the Missouri and rolled slowly toward the Nebraska shore.

"Come on!" a man shouted from Omaha. "Come on!"

Other watchers echoed the cry as the spectators began to take heart.

"We're going to make it, sir!" Donovan breathed, banging Glenn on the shoulder. "Mr. Gilchrist, we're by Gawd goin' to make it!"

"Maybe. But if the ice breaks behind us, the supply cars will drag us into the river. If that happens, we jump and take our chances."

"Yes, sir!" the big Irishman shouted, his square jaw bumping rapidly up and down.

Donovan reeked of whiskey and his eyes were bright and glassy. Glenn turned to look at the young fireman.

"Mr. Chandlis, have you been drinking too?"

"Not a drop, sir." Young Sean Chandlis pointed to shore and cried, "Look, Mr. Gilchrist, we've made it!"

Glenn felt the locomotive bump onto the tracks resting on the solid Nebraska riverbank. Engineer Donovan blasted his steam whistle and nudged the locomotive's throttle, causing the big drivers to spin a little as they surged up the riverbank. Those same sixty-inch driving wheels propelled the supply cars into Omaha where they were enfolded by the jubilant crowd.

The scene was one of pandemonium as Donovan kept yanking on his steam whistle and inciting the crowd. Photographers crowded around the locomotive taking pictures.

"Come on and smile!" Donovan shouted in Glenn's ear. "We're heroes!"

Glenn didn't feel like smiling. His knees wanted to buckle from the sheer relief of having this craziness behind him. He wanted to smash Donovan's grinning face for starting across the river too fast and for drinking on duty. But the photographers kept taking pictures and all that Glenn did was bat Donovan's hand away from the infernal steam whistle before it drove him mad.

God, the warm, fresh chinook winds felt fine on his cheeks and it was good to be still alive. Glenn waved to the crowd and his eyes lifted back to the river that he knew would soon be breaking up if this warm weather held. He turned back to gaze westward and up to the city of Omaha. Omaha—when he'd arrived last fall, it had still been little more than a tiny riverfront settlement. Today, it could boast a population of more than six thousand, all anxiously waiting to follow the Union Pacific rails west.

"We did it!" Donovan shouted at the crowd as he raised his fists in victory. "We did it!"

Glenn saw a tall beauty with reddish hair pushing forward through the crowd, struggling mightily to reach the supply train. "Who is that?"

Donovan followed his eyes. "Why, that's Mrs. Megan Gallagher. Ain't she and her sister somethin', though!"

Glenn had not even noticed the smaller woman with two freckled children in tow who was also waving to the train and trying to follow her sister to its side. Glenn's brow furrowed. "Are their husbands on this supply train?"

Donovan's wide grin dissolved. "Well, Mr. Gilchrist, I know you told everyone that only single men could take this last one across, but . . ."

Glenn clenched his fists in surprise and anger. "Donovan, don't you understand that the Union Pacific made it clear that there was to be no drinking and no married men on this last run! Dammit, you broke both rules! I've got no choice but to fire all three of you."

"But, sir!"

Glenn felt sick at heart but also betrayed. Bill "Wild Man" Donovan was probably the best engineer on the payroll but he'd proved he was also an irresponsible fool, one who played to the crowd and was more than willing to take chances with other men's lives and the Union Pacific's rolling stock and precious construction supplies.

"I'm sorry, Donovan. Collect your pay from the paymaster before quitting time," Glenn said, swinging down from the cab into the pressing crowd. Standing six feet three inches, Glenn was tall enough to look over the sea of humanity and note that Megan

Gallagher and her sister were embracing their triumphant husbands. It made Glenn feel even worse to think that those two men would be without jobs before this day was ended.

Men pounded Glenn on the back in congratulations but he paid them no mind as he pushed through the crowd, moving off toward the levee where these last few vital tons of rails, ties, and other hardware were being stored until the real work of building a railroad finally started.

"Hey!" Donovan shouted, overtaking Glenn and pulling him up short. "You can't fire me! I'm the best damned engineer you've got!"

"*Were* the best," Glenn said, tearing his arm free, "now step aside."

But Donovan didn't budge. The crowd pushed around the two large men, clearly puzzled as to the matter of this dispute in the wake of such a bold and daring success only moments earlier.

"What'd he do wrong?" a man dressed in a tailored suit asked in a belligerent voice. "By God, Bill Donovan brought that train across the river and that makes him a hero in my book!"

This assessment was loudly applauded by others. Glenn could feel resentment building against him as the news of his decision to fire three of the crew swept through the crowd. "This is a company matter. I don't make the rules, I just make sure that they are followed."

Donovan chose to appeal to the crowd. "Now you hear that, folks. Mr. Gilchrist is going to fire three good men without so much as a word of thanks. And that's what the working man gets from this railroad for risking his life!"

"Drop it," Glenn told the big Irishman. "There's nothing left to be gained from this."

"Isn't there?"

"No."

"You're making a mistake," Donovan said, playing to the crowd. The confident Irishman thrust his hand out with a grin. "So why don't we let bygones be bygones and go have a couple of drinks to celebrate? Gallagher and Fox are two of the best men on the payroll. They deserve a second chance. Think about the fact they got wives and children."

Glenn shifted uneasily. "I'll talk to Fox and Gallagher but you were in charge and I hold you responsible."

"Hell, we made it in grand style, didn't we!"

"Barely," Glenn said, "and you needlessly jeopardized the crew and the company's assets, that's why you're still fired."

Donovan flushed with anger. "You're a hard, unforgiving man, Gilchrist."

"And you are a fool when you drink whiskey. Later, I'll hear Fox's and Gallagher's excuses."

"They drew lots for a cash bonus ride across that damned melting river!" Donovan swore, his voice hardening. "Gallagher and Fox needed the money!"

"The Union Pacific didn't offer any bonus! It was your job to ask for volunteers and choose the best to step forward."

Donovan shrugged. He had a lantern jaw, and heavy, fist-scarred brows overhanging a pair of now very angry and bloodshot eyes. "The boys each pitched in a couple dollars into a pot. I'll admit it was my idea. But the winners stood to earn fifty dollars each when we crossed."

"To leave wives and children without support?" Glenn snapped. "That's a damned slim legacy."

"These are damned slim times," Donovan said. "The idea was, if we drowned, the money would be used for the biggest funeral and wake Omaha will ever see. And if we made it . . . well, you saw the crowd."

"Yeah," Glenn said. "If you won, you'd flood the saloons and drink it up so either way all the money would go for whiskey."

"Some to the wives and children," Donovan said quietly.

"Like hell."

Glenn started to turn and leave the man but Donovan's voice stopped him cold. "If you turn away, I'll drop you," the Irishman warned in a soft, all the more threatening voice.

"That would be a real mistake," Glenn said.

Although several inches taller than the engineer, Glenn had no illusions as to matching the Irishman's strength or fighting ability. Donovan was built like a tree stump and was reputed to be one of the most vicious brawlers in Omaha. If Glenn had any advantage, it was that he had been on Harvard's collegiate boxing club and gained some recognition for quickness and a devastating left hook that had surprised and then floored many an opponent.

"Come on, sir," Donovan said with a friendly wink as he reached into his coat pocket and dragged out a pint of whiskey. The engineer uncorked and extended it toward Glenn. "So I got a little carried away out there. No harm, was there?"

"I'm sorry," Glenn said, pivoting around on his heel and starting off toward the levee to oversee the stockpiling and handling of this last vital shipment.

This time when Donovan's powerful fingers dug into
Glenn's shoulder to spin him around, Glenn dropped
into a slight crouch, whirled, and drove his left hook
upward with every ounce of power he could mus-
ter. The punch caught Donovan in the gut. The big
Irishman's cheeks blew out and his eyes bugged.
Glenn pounded him again in the solar plexus and
Donovan staggered, his face turning fish-belly white.
Glenn rocked back and threw a textbook combina-
tion of punches to the bigger man's face that split
Donovan's cheek to the bone and dropped him to his
knees.

"You'd better finish me!" Donovan gasped. " 'Cause
I swear to settle this score!"

Glenn did not take the man's threat lightly. He
cocked back his fist but he couldn't deliver the knock-
out blow, not while the engineer was gasping in agony.
"Stay away from me," Glenn warned before he hurried
away.

He felt physically and emotionally drained by the
perilous river crossing and his fight with Donovan. He
had been extremely fortunate to survive both confron-
tations. It had reinforced the idea in his mind that he
was not seasoned enough to be making such critical
decisions. It wasn't that he didn't welcome responsibility, for he did. But not so much and not so soon.

The trouble was that the fledgling Union Pacific
itself was in over its head. No one knew from one
day to the next whether it would still be in operation
or who was actually in charge. From inception, Vice
President Thomas Durant, a medical doctor turned
railroad entrepreneur, was the driving force behind getting the United States Congress to pass two Pacific
Railway Acts through Congress. With the Civil War

just ending and the nation still numb from the shock of losing President Abraham Lincoln, the long discussed hope of constructing a transcontinental railroad was facing tough sledding. Durant himself was sort of an enigma, a schemer and dreamer who some claimed was a charlatan while others thought he possessed a brilliant organizational mind.

Glenn didn't know what to think of Durant. It had been through him that he'd landed this job fresh out of engineering school as his reward for being his class valedictorian. So far, Glenn's Omaha experience had been nothing short of chaotic. Lacking sufficient funds and with the mercurial Durant dashing back and forth to Washington, there had been a clear lack of order and leadership. It had been almost three years since Congress had agreed to pay both the Union Pacific and the Central Pacific Railroads the sums of $16,000 per mile for track laid over the plains, $32,000 a mile through the arid wastes of the Great Basin, and a whopping $48,000 per mile for track laid over the Rocky and the Sierra Nevada mountain ranges.

Now, with the approach of spring, the stage had been set to finally begin the transcontinental race. One hundred miles of roadbed had been graded westward from Omaha and almost forty miles of temporary track had been laid. For two years, big paddlewheel steamboats had been carrying mountains of supplies up the Missouri River. There were three entire locomotives still packed in shipping crates resting on the levee while two more stood assembled beside the Union Pacific's massive new brick roundhouse with its ten locomotive repair pits. Dozens of hastily constructed shops and offices surrounded the new freight and switching yards.

There was still more work than men and that was a blessing for veterans in the aftermath of the Civil War joblessness and destruction. Every day, dozens more ex-soldiers and fortune seekers crossed the Missouri River into Omaha and signed on with the Union Pacific Railroad. Half a nation away, the Central Pacific Railroad was already attacking the Sierra Nevada Mountains but Glenn had heard that they were not so fortunate in hiring men because of the stiff competition from the rich gold and silver mines on the Comstock Lode.

Glenn decided he would have a few drinks along with some of the other officers of the railroad, then retire early. He was dog-tired and the strain of these last few days of worrying about the stress-carrying capacity of the melting ice had enervated him to the point of bone weariness.

Glenn realized he would be more than glad when the generals finally arrived to take command of the Union Pacific. He would be even happier when the race west finally began in dead earnest.

J.R. ROBERTS

THE
GUNSMITH

If you enjoyed this book, subscribe now and get...

TWO FREE

A $7.00 VALUE—

A special offer for people who enjoy reading the best Westerns published today.

WESTERNS!

NO OBLIGATION

Mail the coupon below

To start your subscription and receive 2 FREE WESTERNS, fill out the coupon below and mail it today. We'll send your first shipment which includes 2 FREE BOOKS as soon as we receive it.

Mail To: **True Value Home Subscription Services, Inc. P.O. Box 5235
120 Brighton Road, Clifton, New Jersey 07015-5235**

YES! I want to start reviewing the very best Westerns being published today. Send me my first shipment of 6 Westerns for me to preview FREE for 10 days. If I decide to keep them, I'll pay for just 4 of the books at the low subscriber price of $2.75 each; a total $11.00 (a $21.00 value). Then each month I'll receive the 6 newest and best Westerns to preview Free for 10 days. If I'm not satisfied I may return them within 10 days and owe nothing. Otherwise I'll be billed at the special low subscriber rate of $2.75 each; a total of $16.50 (at least a $21.00 value) and save $4.50 off the publishers price. There are never any shipping, handling or other hidden charges. I understand I am under no obligation to purchase any number of books and I can cancel my subscription at any time, no questions asked. In any case the 2 FREE books are mine to keep.

Name _____

Street Address _____ Apt. No. _____

City _____ State _____ Zip Code _____

Telephone _____

Signature _____
(if under 18 parent or guardian must sign)

Terms and prices subject to change. Orders subject
to acceptance by True Value Home Subscription
Services Inc.

11105

431